GEMINI BITES

PATRICK RYAN

GEMINI
BITES

SCHOLASTIC PRESS / NEW YORK

All rights reserved. Published by Scholastic Press, an imprint of Scholastic Inc.,
Publishers since 1920. SCHOLASTIC, SCHOLASTIC PRESS, and associated logos are
trademarks and/or registered trademarks of Scholastic Inc.

Library of Congress Cataloging-in-Publication Data available

ISBN 978-0-545-22128-3

10 9 8 7 6 5 4 3 2 1   11 12 13 14 15 16

Printed in the U.S.A. 23

First edition, March 2011

The text type was set in Palatino.

Book design by Christopher Stengel

TO JAMES BLES AND ELIZABETH WEBBER

1. K Y L E :
The biggest exaggerator in
the history of the universe

Sometimes it royally sucks to be a Renneker.

There are nine of us. Nine. Dad, Mom, Tommy, Dexter, Monster (a.k.a. Judy), me, Dawn, Suzie, and Trisha. Having a hard time keeping track? I'd say, "Join the club," but I wouldn't want you to; it's big enough as it is.

Mom and Dad met at an art opening in Richmond, Virginia, fell in love, blah blah blah. They dated for a while, got married, blah blah blah. They had Tommy, and Dexter, and then they had twins—me and Monster. (We're not identical—obviously, because she's a she and I'm a he—but we shared the womb together. This fact still blows my mind, since I can't imagine us sharing a *room*, much less a womb.) Then, when Judy and I were ten, Mom and Dad sat us all down for a "family meeting" and announced they were getting separated. A "trial separation," they called it. There'd been no fighting that any of us had seen, no steamy affairs that we knew of; they'd just fallen out of love "very maturely and with mutual respect." Blah blah *splat*.

Mom and Tommy and I stayed in the house, which suddenly felt like an echo chamber of the life we'd been living; Dad rented an apartment one town over, in Lewiston, and Judy and Dexter went off to live with him.

Supposedly, splitting up twins is the worst thing you can do to them. And, to be honest, when I was ten I still liked Judy. We used to play together. She was, you know, human. But I guess Mom and Dad felt it was only fair for each of them to get half the set, so we were separated for over a year. Dad found some woman named Ellen to date, and Mom found someone else, too—a Buick salesman named Chuck who wasn't mean or overly nice or anything in the extreme. He was just...Chuck. *Chuck the Sleeping Pill*, I called him.

Anyway, a year after Mom and Dad got separated, they were both like, *Why did we ever do that?* and they started seeing each other on the sly. They dumped Ellen and Chuck, respectively, and Dad and the rest of them moved back into the house, followed by a big let's-say-our-vows-again ceremony.

My theory is, if they'd never split up in the first place, they wouldn't have felt the need to have more kids. My theory is, Dawn was the *validation* that Round Two was for real, and Suzie caught them by surprise. As for Trisha, I know for a fact that *she* caught them by surprise, because Mom burst into tears telling Dad about the results of the home pregnancy strip. (I was supposed to have been out of earshot, but wasn't.) Why a little birth control wasn't employed now and then, I have no idea. Yes, we're Catholic, but it's not like we go to church, except for midnight mass at Christmas. And don't get me wrong—I love them all and don't begrudge them their births. It's only that every now and then, I call my own birth into question. Or, at least, my own placement in the lineup. As in: Why do I have to be smack in the middle of this herd?

When Mom and Dad got back together and we were all living in the same old house again, Monster and I were eleven, and she wasn't nice anymore. Not to me. I was all, let's bond in our shared trauma (not really, but still), and she barely even wanted to talk to me. That stuff they say about twins being spiritually close and mentally connected? It sort of clashes with how a human girl can mutate into a creature of incalculable meanness and unpredictable moodiness, not to mention sheer hideousness. As in, her head spinning all the way around. Giant squirts of green puke splattering the walls. Poisonous eels for hair and thorny claws for hands.

But I'm getting ahead of myself. And exaggerating.

A little.

Just so you'll feel like you're receiving a "fair and balanced" picture of Renneker family life, I'll tell you the one significant advantage I've noticed about having six siblings: You can get away with more. Your parents are just too busy to notice everything you do, and there's too much going on for any one event (short of, say, death or a kidnapping) to get that much attention.

Prime example: I knew from around age eleven that I was gay. How did I know? Because guys rocked and girls didn't. Enough said? I kept that little secret for four years—because, really, I felt it was none of my parents' business. But over time this seemed silly, especially since both Mom and Dad had plenty of gay friends who they were clearly cool with. So finally, last year, I decided to follow my friend Ian Heller's lead. Although I hoped for better results.

Ian had recently sat his parents down and said, "You're probably going to be less than thrilled when you hear this, but I can't let that silence me. The truth is that I'm homosexual." Apparently, his mom burst into tears and his dad turned red and wanted to know what they'd done to "cause this." But the world didn't end, and a few weeks later they even made a point of telling him they were working on accepting it. So, after hearing how it went with Ian, and feeling it was ridiculous that he was fully out and I wasn't, I decided to call a family meeting of my own. We gathered in the living room, and I stood in front of the whole brood, cleared my throat, and said these exact words: "Ladies and gentlemen, I'm gay." I even did it with a flourish of my hand, like I was performing a magic trick and *making* myself gay right before their eyes.

Tommy reached over, smacked Dexter's shoulder, and said, "*Told* you. You owe me twenty bucks!"

"What's *gay*?" Trisha asked. She was four at the time.

"Honey," Mom said to me. She looked a little surprised, but I knew she was trying to step up to the plate. "Are you sure?"

"*Oh*, yeah," I said.

"Son," Dad asked, "have you explored this thing at all?"

Dawn made an *eeewww* noise, but you could tell she didn't really care. Tommy smacked Dexter's shoulder and said, "Man, pay *up*."

"What's *gay*?" Trisha asked again.

And then Suzie, who'd carried a big glass of milk into the living room and sat down with it on the couch (against the rules, big-time), let it tip sideways, and a wave of milk fanned out over the cushion. Some of it slid onto Monster's bare leg (she was wearing shorts), and she started howling.

"Oh, *Suzie*!" Mom snapped, and ran to the kitchen for paper towels.

Dexter reached for the remote; Dawn asked if she could eat just the strawberry stripe out of the Neapolitan ice cream; Dad suggested using baking soda to get the milk smell out of the cushion.

Wah-lah: gay crisis over. Mom and Dad had six other kids to worry about. The fact that guys turned me on just didn't make their daily list of concerns.

Now all I needed was a boyfriend.

Monster was pretty silent about my being gay—at least at first. But she wasn't silent about much else.

In our family, competition is the rule. It has to be.

If dinner is pork chops and there are nine chops on the serving plate, *one* of them, according to physics, is the smallest—but it isn't the smallest kid who gets it; it's the slowest. On Christmas Day, it isn't the most well-behaved kid who gets the best presents; it's the one who's been the loudest about what he or she wants in the months leading up to the holiday. And Monster was the worst of all—especially when it came to competing with *me*.

Take the time she wanted a laptop. Even though there was already a computer in the house with internet access (sitting on a table outside the pantry, privacy not an option), she said she *needed* a laptop because of all the papers she had to write for her Advanced English class. For a while that laptop was all she talked about. She could pay for half of it, she said, with the money from her job at Starbucks but, boy, she sure could use some family help in collecting the rest of the amount. And then she played the trump card. She told Mom and Dad that all of us could *share* the laptop anytime one of us needed it, and that was all they needed to hear. There it was, delivered by UPS, and where did that sleek new laptop always seem to be? In Monster's room, of course. And had I ever even sat down in front of it? Twice—once to help her set it up, and once to read an email from our grandfather in Fort Lauderdale ("Hi, Judy. Tell all your brothers and sisters we said HELLO!"). She hovered over me as I read it, and when I asked if I could respond, she said, "When I'm done with my schoolwork," and then spent the next two hours on YouTube.

Competition.

When I was fourteen, I broke a bone in my forearm playing basketball, and I swear, as soon as Judy got a look at me in my cast and saw the attention I was getting from Mom and Dad and everyone else, she contracted mononucleosis on the spot. They call it "mono" for short, but they ought to call it "Kiss My Lazy Butt" because Monster didn't have to lift a finger around the house for weeks. I, on the other hand, with one arm in a cast, had to vacuum her room.

"I win," she'd say, dashing into the bathroom right as I was about to use it, and then slam the door in my face.

"I win!" she'd cheer after yanking the remote out of my hand.

"*I* win. Not you. *Me*," she'd all but snarl if she'd complained that my music was too loud and Mom had made me turn it down.

"Not *every*thing's a competition," Mom would sometimes remind us.

But she was wrong. Everything was.

I envied Ian, who had no brothers or sisters, who didn't even have a dog (or a houseplant). It was just him and his parents. And they spoiled him, gave him whatever he asked for, and took him to Paris and Madrid in the summers. Not that any of this made Ian a happy camper. He was a good friend, but he was the most cynical person I'd ever known. "You *don't* want to be me," he said one afternoon, when I told him I'd rather be a

Heller than a Renneker. "Imagine sitting down to dinner every evening of your life, and you've got one of two choices: You either listen to your parents talk to each other about work, or you play twenty questions about what's going on with *you*. You get up in the middle of the night to pee, and your mom comes out and asks if you're all right because she heard a floorboard squeak. You tell them you're gay, and they look at you—their only child—like you've just deliberately erased all their future grandchildren from existence. Hello? Who would want to bring a child into this world? It we don't blow it up first, global warming's going to get us."

"I'm just saying, it would be nice to live in a more...focused... home. And it would be nice not to have a sister who's got it in for you night and day," I said.

"Plus," he said, "if you were me, you'd have this body, and this hair."

I looked him up and down. He wasn't a small kid, by any means, but he wasn't oversize, either. "What's wrong with your body?" I asked. "You look fine."

"You've never seen me without clothes. Naked, I look like a ziplock bag filled with cottage cheese."

"You do not!" I said. "That's crazy."

"Everyone in my family becomes larger with each passing year. What's to be done about it?"

"Um, diet?" I suggested. (He was right; his parents were huge.)

"It's in the genes."

"Well, what's wrong with your hair?" He had a full mop of curly brown hair that made him look, from a distance, like he was wearing a Russian fur hat.

"Again, it's in the genes. Males get their hair from their mother's father. My mother's father looked like a cue ball by the time he was thirty."

I thought of Granddad Whitmore, on Mom's side. He still had hair—it was white and thinning a little, but it was still there. More than Dad's was, that's for sure. I considered myself lucky. "There's always a toupee," I said.

"And that, my friend, is my future: a fat, bald man with a rug. Which is why, as soon as I can, I'm going to flee this cow town and move to New York so I can have a little fun before the Genetic Express runs me down."

"And your parents will probably bankroll it because they don't have *six other kids* to feed and put through college."

"They *won't* bankroll it. But they'll call every night, and they'll want updates, and they'll want me home for every single holiday on the calendar, because it's just *solo mío*, the only child they've got."

I told him he should consider himself lucky.

"Person who prefers his own sex to the sex of females," Judy said one evening, sticking her head into my room, "Mom says to remind you you're the pre-dinner helper tonight."

Monster was constantly coming up with new things to call me when our parents were out of earshot. She wouldn't call me "fag" or anything bad like that, but she could really get creative with her labels. These seemed to get only more sharp and consistent after her religious conversion (which came close on the heels of my coming out—the broken arm and the mono, all over again).

A few months ago, out of the blue, she called us all together and claimed she'd been saved.

"Saved from...?" Mom asked.

"The Devil," Monster said. "Satan. Life everlasting in the flames of damnation. I've found the Lord."

"Please," I said, and Mom shot me a look; she put up with a lot from us, but she didn't like it when we made fun of one another—at least, not in front of her.

"Judy," Dad said, stammering a little. Then he asked, "Have you...explored this thing at all?"

Perfect, right? Well done. Score one for Monster.

She hung a wooden cross on the wall over her bed. She hung a picture of Jesus—not one of those ones with the blinking eyes, thank God—above her dresser and started carrying a bible around with her everywhere she went. She was probably the only person on Earth who could undergo a complete religious conversion and yet stay mean—to me, anyway. She was as mean as ever, only now she had Jesus backing her.

I was sitting on my bed with my guitar, practicing the chord progression for "Don't Think Twice, It's All Right."

"Tell Mom I'll be down in a minute, would you?" I said.

"You tell her, butt-ranger," Monster said. "I have to finish my reading." She wagged her bible at me. It had tiny print and was about as big as a Fig Newton.

"Seeing Jacob tonight?"

"I have bible study. So, yes, I'm seeing Jacob."

Jacob Lindsey had dark red hair, a gorgeous face, and these really soft-looking lips I wouldn't have minded kissing for about, oh, ten hours. He was ultraserious and jockish, though, and I was pretty sure he didn't have a pew at my church.

"Good luck with your reading," I told her, glancing at the bible.

"I don't need luck, heathen," she said. "I have the Lord on my side."

"And that's why you're the Holiest Monster at Milton High," I said.

"And that's why *you're* the Boy Who Loves Penises."

As if the two things were even remotely connected. I groaned, reached over to my stereo, and hit the PLAY button. "Like a Rolling Stone" blasted out of the speakers, filling the air between us, and Bob Dylan started singing.

About Dylan: I wanted to know him (now), I wanted to be him (always), and I wanted to *do* him (via time machine, circa 1965). I'd started listening to him after my friend Brian Sutton put on "Subterranean Homesick Blues" one afternoon when I was over at his house. I had a crush on Brian Sutton (I have a lot of crushes) and wanted to like anything he liked. But the more I listened, the more I actually did like it. The song was crazy—in a good way. It was edgy and in-your-face. Dylan sounded like he was singing through his nose, but so what? He was obviously cool, and what I didn't tell Brian Sutton, who was straight and wouldn't have understood, was that Bob Dylan, on that album cover and in every other picture I'd seen of him from that time period, was *hot*. So I started buying his music. It was all over the map—love ballads and folk songs, rock and country-western, songs about girls mouthing off and songs about being saved—and while some of it was weird, *most* of it was mind-blowing. Not long after I became a certified Dylanhead, I found a box of actual records at a garage sale and bought the whole thing for five dollars. There must have been twenty Dylan records in there. Not that I had a record player to play any of them on, but inside the sleeve of the *Greatest Hits* album I found this folded, perfectly preserved poster, a drawing of him in profile with his hair rendered in all kinds of crazy colors, and that's what was taped up over *my* dresser (not Jesus, thank you).

No one in the family got it. Dexter, whose musical tastes centered mainly around that moronic "la-la-la-la...*HEY!*" song they always play at football games, would put his hands over his ears if he was passing my room and I was playing Dylan. "Aren't you supposed to be listening to Judy Garland or something like that?"

"Why, because I'm gay?"

"That'd be a yeah."

"He's singing about what's *real*," I'd say. "He's singing about what's *true*."

"He's singing about a leopard-skin hat."

I didn't care what anyone else thought. And when I bought an acoustic guitar at the pawn shop, taught myself some basic chords, and started figuring out how to play some of Dylan's songs, I didn't play for anyone but me—and that was fine. Sometimes I pretended I was him. Sometimes I pretended he was sitting across from me on my bed, listening to me play, totally into me and giving me that *I-know-what-you're-about* look.

They call it a fantasy for a reason, you know?

On the night that everything massively, unalterably, confoundingly, stupendously changed, dinner was baked chicken, mixed vegetables, and iced tea. I stabbed my fork into the biggest drumstick I could spot and dragged it onto my plate.

"My Poli-Sci professor's a total nutcase," Tommy said, scratching his fingers over the goatee he was trying to grow. "He actually told the class he had Montezuma's revenge today and was ending the lecture early. Is that disgusting, or what?"

Dexter said, "Shut up!" in that way that didn't mean *shut up* but *no way!*

"I don't like chicken," Suzie said. It was her newest thing—claiming she didn't like whatever we were about to eat.

"You *love* chicken," Mom told her.

"I'm serious!" Tommy said. "That's what he said. Montezuma's revenge!"

Dawn thumped her fork against her knife and said, "That's disgusting." Each of her fingers and both her thumbs were wrapped in aluminum foil; I didn't ask.

"Honey," Mom said, looking at Dad down the length of the table, "can't you read later, when we're not eating?"

"I'm almost done with this chapter," Dad said without looking up.

"I can borrow the car tonight, right?" Monster asked. "Somebody's?"

"I need mine," Dad said. "I'm going to Home Depot, if anyone wants to come along."

"Tommy? Can I borrow your car?"

"What for?"

"I have bible study tonight. It's usually Saturday but this is a Tuesday night special meeting."

"Didn't you hear?" Tommy asked. "God is dead."

"Tommy!" Mom huffed. I was pretty sure she herself believed only in the random collision of molecules, but like I said, she didn't want us making fun of one another.

"God is *not* dead," Monster told him. "Please, can I borrow your car? I'll put gas in it."

"What's *Monty Zooma's Revenge*?" Trisha asked.

"A loosening of the stool," Dexter offered, and all of us old enough to know that a stool wasn't necessarily a piece of furniture made gross-out noises.

"Dexter," Mom said.

"You can borrow my car," Tommy told Monster. "Just don't, you know, baptize it or anything."

"What are you reading, anyway?" Mom asked.

"Can chickens swim?" Suzie asked.

Case Studies in Clinical Depression," Dad said. (He's a psychologist, so this almost made sense.) "And I am now done with my chapter." He closed the book. "What was that about Montezuma's revenge?"

"We've moved on," Mom told him. "So what's the destination for Junior Jaunt this year?"

Junior Jaunt was a field trip the juniors got to take once a year. (There were also Sophomore Jaunt and Senior Jaunt, but they didn't sound quite as ridiculous without the alliteration.)

"Colonial Williamsburg," Monster told Mom, and rolled her eyes. "The seniors get to go to Kings Dominion. Tell me that's fair."

"Sounds fair to me," said Dexter, who was a senior. Then he started listing all the rides he could remember from the very few times our family had gone to Kings Dominion over the years. (Dad hated amusement parks.) Dexter ranked the rides 1–10 in terms of how cool they were, and described the new roller coaster, which he said was *definitely* a 10 from the commercials he'd seen.

I was sitting across from Monster. She was scowling as she listened to Dexter, and she was chewing with her mouth open; you could see the chicken just rolling around in there. I got her attention, pointed at her, and then pointed to my own mouth.

She smirked and said, "Did you just ask me to kiss you?"

"No! I was trying to tell you—" *that you eat like a wood chipper,* I was about to say, but Mom interrupted me.

"Kyle, don't talk with your mouth full."

She was right; I had food in my mouth. I swallowed, and before I could say anything else, Judy gave me a sly smile and mouthed, *I win.*

"I have an announcement to make," Dexter said to the group at large.

"So do I," Dad said.

"So do I!" Trisha said, and then burped as loudly as she could.

"Excuse you," Mom scolded.

"Excuse me," Trisha sang, darting her eyes around the table.

"Why don't you go first?" Dad said to Dexter. "Everyone, focus. Dexter would like to share something with us."

Suddenly, dinner had turned into a family meeting. Family meetings were almost never as interesting as "I'm gay," and usually as boring as, "No tennis shoes in the dryer." Dexter sniffed loudly and stared down at his food. "I'm not going to college next year," he said.

Mom's fork connected with her plate. "What?"

"I've decided to take a year off. Make some money." We were a month away from the end of the school year, which meant Dexter was a month away from graduating.

"But you've already been accepted," Mom said.

"U.Va.'s not going anywhere. If I stay here and take the job Mac Prentice is offering me at Athletic Mongoose, I can bank the money, and then go away to college next year."

Dad groaned. His face went slack except for his raised eyebrows, which wrinkled the dome of his forehead. He looked at Mom and said, "They're never going to move out, are they? None of them. We're stuck with them forever."

"Don't make jokes," Mom said. "This is serious." She turned back to Dexter. "So Mac Prentice is giving career advice? I don't think he even made it out of middle school."

"Yeah, and now he owns his own franchise. Pretty impressive, if you ask me."

"Dex," Tommy said, "why don't you just commute, like I do? It's a cinch."

"Because I don't *want* to commute. Because the whole point is that I don't want to go to college right now. I want to make some money."

"Would you have to take the SAT all over again?" I asked. Dexter had barely scraped by on his SAT and had claimed that taking it was one of the suckiest days of his life. It was pretty obvious from his expression now that he hadn't thought about that part.

"All right," Dad said, "let's look at this realistically. What are the chances, Dexter—and I really want you to think about this—what are the chances that, a year from now, you might decide you *still* don't want to go to school?"

Dexter shrugged. "I'm not Nostradamus."

"Nor am I. But what's going to make college look more attractive in a year than it does right now? Especially if you've been putting money in the bank?"

"Maybe it *won't* look more attractive."

"You have to get a college degree," Mom said.

"Or," Dad said, raising an index finger the way he did whenever he had an *important point* to make, "you could work at Athletic Mouse—"

"*Mongoose*," Dexter corrected.

"—Mongoose for the next five, who knows, maybe ten years..."

"And get nowhere in life," Mom cut in.

Trisha burped again and sang, "Excuse me." We all ignored her.

"*Those* are my two choices?" Dexter asked. "People do all *kinds* of things with their lives."

Mom nodded. "And people make bad decisions every day."

"Well, what about 'learn from your mistakes'? You're always telling me that."

"If you already know it's a mistake, then why on Earth would you do it?"

"I don't understand why I have to feel so boxed in," Dexter said. "I have options."

"Like what?"

"I could go to a vocational school anytime I wanted. Or sign up for the peace corps. Or...join the military."

"Whoa!" Dad snapped. "Don't go off the deep end, now. Let's just stay focused."

We "stayed focused" through the end of dessert. I spent the rest of the meal thinking about how I liked it better when there were Ping-Pong balls flying all over the table.

Just as we were about to get up (I wasn't on cleanup duty because I'd been on pre-dinner-help detail), Tommy said, "Wait, Dad never made *his* announcement."

"That's right," Dad said. "I never did."

Dad loved an audience. We all looked at him, and he just stared back at us for a few moments, then cleared his throat and said, "Actually, it's a double announcement. A two-parter. Part the first: The game room will be finished by this coming weekend. I'm putting the last coat of paint on it this week."

Trisha hoorayed and Suzie, Dawn, and Judy clapped. Tommy and Dexter and I high-fived one another. The game room had been Dad's ongoing project for months. He'd hired carpenters and drywall guys to come in and finish off the half of the attic we weren't using for storage, and his original plan had been to turn it into a kind of study area where we could all do our homework after school. (Hello? Why not just turn it into a dentist's office?) But then he'd gotten a really good deal on a giant flat-screen TV, and suddenly he had the idea of turning the space into a game room. He bought a chess set, a backgammon set, a dartboard. Then he got, as he put it, "obsessive" about things. He went on eBay, and within a few weeks he'd found an air hockey table, a pinball machine that was about a hundred years old (well, okay, it was from the early '80s), and—how cool is this?—a Ms. Pac-Man *and* a Galaga game. All that stuff had already been delivered and was sitting in giant boxes in the attic. We'd been forbidden to step foot up there until he was done. (He didn't want any help and had told us outright that the project had been conceived to give him some alone time.) We'd been waiting and waiting for him to finish. The day was finally approaching.

"What's the other announcement?" I asked.

"Part the second: We're going to have a visitor. A guest in our house."

"Who?"

"His name is Garret Johnson."

My mouth dropped open. I couldn't help it—I looked at Monster. But she was frowning at the table.

"His father is—or was—in my runners' club," Dad went on. "Hal's a prefab-housing plant manager, and he's been transferred to a new San Diego branch that's about to open up. Garret's a student at Milton." He glanced at me. "Maybe you and Judy know him?"

I knew *of* him, that was for sure. I'd seen him around.

"Why us?" I asked.

"He's in your class. He's a junior."

Monster said nothing; I followed her lead.

"In any event," Dad said, "because the end of the school year is just four weeks away, your mother and I have offered to take

Garret in so he can finish the year off here at Milton, rather than having to relocate to a new school so late in the game."

"He's going to be staying with us for a *month*?" Suzie asked.

"Almost to the day. And unless any of you with a single room feels like sharing your space, he's going to be staying in the attic."

"Nooo!" Trisha cried. You would have thought someone had lopped off her hand.

"Yeeesss," Dad said. "So the new game room won't be officially 'in business' till the school year is out, because it will be Garret's living quarters. Unless, that is, he feels like inviting you up. And I want you all to do your best to make him feel welcome. Understood?"

Welcome. I could tell by Monster's expression that she'd gotten a look at this guy, too. Garret Johnson was in both my American History and gym classes, and he was one of the strangest kids at Milton. He was as pale as a ghost. He wore eyeliner—but only on *one* eye. His black hair hung in this crazy shag over his forehead, and his clothes were nearly all black. He carried around a giant sketchbook and sat with it in the Commons, drawing people. The only time I'd heard him speak was on the first day of class when the history teacher had asked each of us to say our name. When it came around to Garret, he'd said in a dry, icy voice, "The name's Garret. As opposed to *garrote*, the device one might use to strangle a person."

I wondered if Dad had actually met this kid, face-to-face.

"That reminds me," Mom said. "Can you pick up another laundry basket when you're at the Home Depot? And a Sharpie? Someone left the cap off mine and it dried out." She ran her eyes around the table, searching for a guilty face.

"Will do," Dad said. "So we're all clear on that, then. Garret — our guest — will be an official resident here on Saturday."

"The first day the game room is open," Tommy muttered.

"Or not," Dexter added.

Just what we need, I thought. *One more person in the house. And a freak, to boot.*

2. J U D Y :
In pursuit of a boyfriend,
God willing

P ay no attention to the rumors. I'm a lovely person. I'm one of the nicest people in Milton; just ask anyone but Kyle. Well, maybe don't ask Tommy or Dexter, because they'll only say something sarcastic. And don't ask Dawn or Suzie, either, because they'll try to be funny and whatever they say will be stupid, trust me. And if you ask Trisha, who's too young to know whether or not a person is truly nice, chances are she'll just burp.

Ask my dad. He might bore you to tears with my entire psychological profile by way of an answer, but he'll tell you how nice I am. And my mom is the safest bet of all; she couldn't stand the thought of having *any*one in the family who wasn't nice to the nth power.

Kyle, on the other hand, will tell you I'm mean as a snake. And I am, when it comes to him. I can't help it.

I don't like him. And no matter what he says, he started it. The not-liking part, I mean.

He passed me in the upstairs hallway that night just as I was getting ready to leave. He said, "This kid Garret's a real weirdo—you know that, right?"

"All I know," I said, tucking my bible into my purse, "is that I'm running late, and you're a dick-sniffer. But hate the sin, not the sinner, as they say."

"He's *scary*," Kyle said. "You've seen him. He wears eye makeup like those guys in *A Clockwork Orange*."

"So maybe he's half a drag queen. Which might make him half a fellow dick-sniffer. You should be at least *half* thrilled that he's going to be staying here."

Kyle's entire face reset itself in a kind of dazed way, as if, for just a second, he *was* half thrilled. He said, "I can't believe Dad's going to let this guy stay with us for a whole month. And in the *game* room."

"Whatever. Jesus calls."

I have to admit, I really didn't get the whole game room enthusiasm. I just didn't understand what was so exciting about video games and a big-screen TV. I mean, how much fun could it be, wasting time on a Ms. Pac-Man machine, or watching a movie that was four times as large as it was on a regular TV screen but still a *hundredth* as large as it was in a movie theater?

I had a much higher calling.

I steered Tommy's Volkswagen down Filmont Street until I

got to Ironworks Boulevard. Have you ever heard that expression, "the wrong side of the tracks"? There was the nice part of Milton—where we lived—and the not-so-nice part: the wrong side of the tracks. You literally had to cross over the railroad tracks to get to it.

I'm not like Kyle; I don't blow everything out of proportion, so I won't say this part of town is dangerous or even seedy. It's just kind of...ugly. There's a whole stretch of road where half the businesses are either boarded up and covered with graffiti or just empty, as if all the people vanished overnight. And I don't know what's up with the garbagemen, but they don't seem too interested in picking up the trash on a regular basis in this part of town. I turned on the radio and rolled the dial away from Tommy's heavy metal station, trying to find something a little more Christian.

And then it was as if I'd jinxed myself, because the dial slid right into a Christian country song where this woman was belting out, "You can keep your Ford, I've got the love of the Lord...."

I *zoomed* past that one—Jesus is no excuse for artistic lameness—and kept turning till I hit a nice, upbeat love song.

One dumpy building after another passed by. Finally I got to Ryland Drive. Which led to Compton Street (turn left at the dead refrigerator). Which led right up to the gravel driveway of the one and only Jacob Lindsey.

Ah, Jacob.

J.A.C.O.B. (Just a cute ol' boy!)

I'd first laid eyes on him at a pep rally and had been aching for him ever since. It took three weeks of passing him in the halls in between classes to get his attention. It took a week after that to get him not to freak out when I smiled and said hi. The first time he finally said hi back instead of just nodding, he sounded like he was shivering: "H-h-h-h-hi."

He wasn't like that with his guy friends. He played on the football team and hung out with a lot of jocks and could be just as loud as any of them when they were horsing around in the hallways. But whenever I got within ten feet of him, he turned to ice.

"Do you think he's like Kyle?" I asked my best friend, Sasha, after yet another shiver session.

"What do you mean? A Dylan freak?"

"A ho-mo-sex-u-al."

Sasha shrieked. She was always shrieking. Say all you want about us dumb blondes; she was a dumber-than-dumb brunette. "I forgot about that! Oh my God! Do you think Kyle actually has sex with boys?"

"I don't care if he has sex with llamas. I'm talking about *Jacob*. Do you think he might be gay?"

"No," Sasha said. "But I can never tell who's gay and who isn't. They should have to wear something that says what they are."

"Like a pink star? Brilliant."

"Yeah—a pink star! That would be cool and kind of... fashionable."

See what I mean? She should just go ahead and *dye* her hair blond.

I snagged Jacob in the cafeteria one day when he was walking away from the cash register with his lunch tray in his hands. Grinning at him like we'd been sharing dirty secrets for half our lives, I walked right up, touched his arm, and said, "Hi, cutie."

He jumped. I thought he was going to be wearing his lunch any second, but then he pulled himself together and coughed one of those fake coughs people do when they don't know what to say. Goofy, but sexy-goofy.

"Hi," he finally managed.

"So when are you going to ask me out?"

"Ask you...?"

"Out," I said. "Like, out somewhere. On a date."

"Oh. Um...I don't know?"

"Well, you should decide," I said. "We've been flirting with each other for about a month now."

He looked down at the food on his tray and stammered.

"How about this Saturday?" I suggested.

"Well, Saturday nights I have a kind of...standing engagement."

A girlfriend, I thought. *He has a girlfriend, duh. Why did that never occur to me?*

But then he added, "I sort of host a study group."

Had I heard that right? A study group? On *Saturday night*?

I shrugged and said, "I like to study."

"Well, it's a bible study."

Ho. Lee. Crap. Just then I caught sight of maybe the one detail on his whole body I'd never noticed before: a gold chain around his neck with a tiny gold cross dangling from it. You could have swallowed that cross without noticing, it was so tiny. "You're serious," I said. The words were out of my mouth before I could stop them.

"Yeah."

What now? I thought. *How in the world can someone so cute be a...be a...*

And then I realized it only made him cuter.

"I *love* the bible!" I told him.

"You do?"

"Yes! I think it's fascinating. Really. I mean, all those stories."

"Do you have..." He lowered his voice as if we were talking about drugs or something worse. "...a *personal* relationship with...your Savior?"

I bit the insides of my cheeks and checked myself. I didn't want to make fun of him; I wanted to *land* him.

"No," I said decisively, trying to sound regretful. "But I *feel* Him, you know? I mean, I read the bible and I *get* it. I mean, I *get* what's going on. It's all about good and evil, and how good is obviously the better choice and evil is—bad!" Forget Sasha; I was beginning to sound like the blonde I was.

But he smiled at me for the first time.

I said, "I just feel like, I don't know, if I could get to know the bible better, I might get closer to...my Savior."

You're probably wondering right about now if I'm going to hell for lying like this to a good Christian boy. I might be. I'll send you a smoking postcard if that's the case, because what mattered on the spot was that it *worked*. Jacob Lindsey looked me right in the eye and said, "You should come to my study. It's at my house. It would be great if you could be there."

And at that moment, I actually felt something sort of like God. Because it seemed like nothing but divine intervention had set me and Jacob up.

"He's a Jesus freak!" I told Sasha that night.

She screeched into the phone. It sounded like someone was shoving a squirrel into a pipe. "And you can be his Mary! Oh, wait. That was his mom, wasn't it?"

"Isn't it crazy? Someone that cute who has *God* as his main love interest?"

"I dated a Seventh-day Adventist in the eighth grade," she said. "Did you know those people aren't allowed to do *anything* on Saturdays? Anything that might be considered work, I mean. I told him I thought it was great because he never had to worry about doing homework on a Saturday. His name was Nelson, and he had the most gorgeous eyes...but in the end, I guess he thought that *I* was too much work, too."

"*Sasha*. Earth to ditz. Focus."

"Okay, okay. So what are you going to do?"

"I know *exactly* what I'm going to do. I'm going to go for it. He's so nervous around me, you know? I thought he was going to have a heart attack when he introduced himself. I mean, what's it, like, a sin to tell a girl your name?"

"But what do you mean, 'go for it'?"

"I'm going to get saved!"

Screech, screech.

"I am!" I told her. "Not really, of course, but if I act like it's real and start attending his bible study, he'll have no choice but to get to know me. And then I'm in."

"How are you going to pull *that* off?"

"I don't know. I guess I'll have to start reading the bible and, like, pray or something."

"Don't get all high and mighty on me," Sasha said. "If you really do find Jesus, I don't want you, like, walking around in a nun outfit and quoting scripture."

I remembered this great magnet I'd seen in a card shop in DC once. It said, I FOUND JESUS—HE WAS HIDING BEHIND THE SOFA THIS WHOLE TIME! I considered telling her about it, but didn't want her screeching in my ear again. "I don't plan on becoming a fanatic, if that's what you mean. But, really, how hard can it be to fake it?"

"Well, if anyone can pull it off, you can," she said.

I wasn't sure if that was a compliment or not, but I let it go.

♊

The usual cars were parked in front of the Lindsey house, along with a bright yellow convertible I'd never seen before. I rolled the VW up behind the convertible and killed the lights.

The house was small—maybe a tenth the size of ours. We weren't rich, and I don't think the Lindseys were poor, but there was a huge difference between our two families. For one thing, there were nine of us, and with the Lindseys it was just Jacob and his dad. (Mr. and Mrs. Lindsey were divorced and Jacob had told me his mom lived in North Carolina and was remarried.) For another thing, while I didn't exactly feel like soul mates with either of my parents, there was a *huge* disconnect between Jacob and his dad, which was that he was saved and his dad wasn't (and that bothered Jacob to no end). Mr. Lindsey was a roofer who worked Monday through Saturday and drank beer in the evenings. (No Seventh-day Adventist, that one.)

I put on what I thought of as the rubberhead (my mega-calm, mega-sincere, and mega-pleasant expression) and rang the doorbell.

This was my tenth bible study, and the group had always been the same: just Jacob, me, a boy named Dwayne, and a mousy little girl named Noelle. But this time a new girl answered the door.

She was...What's the best way to describe her? I want to say ugly, or at least gross. Unfortunately, neither of those things was true. She was pretty. In fact, she looked like a model. She had high cheekbones, full lips, and brown hair that hung down almost to her skinny little waist. And it's not that I'm short, by any means, but she was nearly a foot taller than me. I could hear the others inside talking about Junior Jaunt while she stood there blocking the doorway, her long-lashed eyes narrowing just a bit as she took me in. Then she said, "Hello. I'm Tina. You must be..."

You could tell she didn't have any idea who I *must be*. "Judy," I told her. "Judy Renneker."

"Judy," she said. "Of course. Welcome."

Uh-huh. And why the hell are you answering Jacob's door?

"Nice T-shirt," she said as I stepped past her.

"Thanks."

She let out a breathy little laugh. "I was being sarcastic."

I'd just gotten the shirt that afternoon, specifically to wear to bible study. It was light blue, and across the front of it, it said, JESUS IS COMING. LOOK BUSY.

I didn't care whether she liked my shirt or not. But then it dawned on me that maybe the shirt was supposed to be funny. Shit! I'd just seen the word *Jesus* and had carried it to the register at T-Shirt World (sort of the same way I'd speed-shopped my way through the religious supply store two months ago). Was *Look busy* a joke? Of course it was—it seemed so obvious, now that this girl was staring at me.

There was nothing to do but play it serious. "I got this at Saving Grace," I lied.

"Weird," Tina said.

"Actually, there's nothing weird about it." I walked straight through the living room into the den, where Jacob and the others were sitting. "Hi!" I said brightly. "Do you like my new shirt?"

"Hi," Jacob said, getting up from his chair. He was smiling, but his smile leveled off when he read the shirt, and he looked a little confused. "Um..."

"Tina thinks it's supposed to be funny," I said, as if Tina and I were already pals, "but it's not. It's *very* serious. I mean, you wouldn't want to look *lazy* if Jesus showed up, would you?"

"No, I...I guess not," Jacob said.

I walked over to him and gave him a hug. He smelled like a cupcake. Then, because it was one of those everyone-has-to-feel-good-about-himself groups, I hugged everyone else. Dwayne smelled like baloney.

"Do you go to Milton?" I asked Tina.

"No. I go to Barrendale."

"So how do you know Jacob?" I tried to sound as if I was just making conversation and couldn't have cared less.

"Tina and I both go to First Baptist," Jacob said.

She smiled her perfect model smile. "Where do *you* go?"

"I'm...between churches right now."

"We're just about to get started," Jacob told me.

"Great," I said, opening my purse and pulling out my bible. "I'm ready. One hundred percent."

We pulled the chairs into a circle. Tina planted her butt down on the one next to Jacob's, and I tried my rubberhead-best not to glare at her.

"Let's begin with a prayer," Jacob said. He held his hands out to either side, and Tina took one, Noelle the other. I was stuck between Noelle and Dwayne, whose hand felt like a damp flipper.

Jacob closed his eyes. So did the rest of them. I closed mine but immediately reopened them to look at Jacob. "Father," he began—and just then, his dad called from upstairs:

"Jacob? Do you have the sports page?"

I thought that was hilarious. He says the word *father*, and his dad starts hollering. But I didn't allow myself to laugh.

"No!" Jacob called back. "We're doing our bible study, Dad!"

"Oh. Sorry."

"Father—" Jacob began again.

"If you see it, don't throw it out!" his dad hollered. "I haven't read it yet!"

Jacob let his mouth hang open for a minute, then called, *"All right!"* He cleared his throat. Everyone but me shut their eyes again. "Father, we pray that You bless us tonight, help us learn more about Your teachings, and guide us as we go out into the world and share Your message. Amen."

Right. I wasn't too big on sharing. I didn't want to share Jacob with anyone, that was for sure.

"Okay," he said, opening his eyes, "why don't we turn to this week's reading, the book of Job?"

This, of course, was my least favorite part of bible study: the bible. Worse, still, Jacob asked *me* if I would read the first two chapters out loud, which stank because not only did I have to pay attention but I couldn't look at him. I smiled and said, "Sure," and held up the book. " 'The book of Job, chapter one. There was a man in the land of...Ooze?...whose name was Job....' "

Fascinating stuff (not). When I finished reading, we talked for a while about what it all *meant*, about what kind of person Job was, and about what it would be like to suddenly lose everything.

"I think Job was amazing," Tina said. "I could only hope to be that strong."

"Me, too," Jacob said.

Dwayne and Noelle weighed in, agreeing.

Jacob asked, "What do you think, Judy?"

"Raw deal," I said. "They really jerked him around, don't you think?"

The rest of them looked at me like I wasn't getting it.

"But...the Lord works in mysterious ways," I added, "and I agree with everyone else. Job was amazing." I hated that my brain latched on to the same word Tina had used.

I hated Tina.

We spent a half hour talking about those two crummy chapters, and then another half hour talking about whether or not we thought God and Satan ever had philosophical debates about *us*. Um, who cares, as long they don't blow the house down? I watched Jacob's biceps flex when he moved his arms, watched him flip his gorgeous hair out of his eyes, watched his lips slide wetly against each other while he was thinking about what he wanted to say.

This was worth it, right? I had to believe in at least *that* much.

"Laundry!" Mom called from the living room when I was half-way up the stairs.

I turned around and stomped back down to the first floor. My basket, the name *Judy* written across the handle, was waiting for me in the laundry room. I grabbed it and hauled it upstairs.

Kyle was in my room, using the laptop. "Get out," I told him, dropping the basket onto the bed.

"Hello? I'm finishing my homework."

"You're on the internet."

"I'm emailing my English composition paper to myself. It's a very sensible way to make backup files."

I kicked my shoes off and thought about throwing one of them at his head. But I didn't want to risk hurting the laptop. "You've got two minutes."

"What's the matter with you?"

"I'm in a bad mood and don't feel like putting up with your crap, all right?"

"Boy," he said, "bible study really brings out the best in you."

Actually, for the first time, it had done the opposite. It was never a thrill (except for the being-around-Jacob part), but I'd had big plans to stick around once everyone else had left—see if I could get ol' Jacob to loosen up a little, get his mind off the bible and onto me. But that bitch Tina *wouldn't budge*. Noelle was out the door because she had to finish a science project. Dwayne left soon after because he had an early curfew. (Imagine having an early curfew and spending what free time you had at a bible study.) But Tina? She was far too busy batting her eyes at Jacob and rambling on about Job to get her ass up and leave. I tried to wait her out, but even *I* had a curfew and had to be home by ten-thirty, so finally I gave up. I couldn't admit any of this to Kyle, of course, because it would have blown my cover. I had big plans for Jacob: boyfriend plans. Which meant one day—soon, I hoped—being able to have him over to the house to hang out (something told me I might get a little further with him in my room than in his). Which meant the family couldn't know I was faking the religious thing, or at least *one* of them would blow my cover.

"Don't you have something gay to do?" I snapped at Kyle. "Somewhere else?"

"Hey, look at this." He pulled last year's yearbook out from under his English reader and flipped it open to a page marked with a Post-it note.

From several feet away, I peered at the picture he was pointing to. "Who is it?"

"*What* is it, is more like it. Look. You have to see it up close."

I walked over to the desk, jerked the book out of his hands, and looked at the picture. It was Garret Johnson's headshot. "So what?"

"So what? Look at the guy! He looks like a total nutcase."

He didn't. His chin was tilted slightly upward, his black hair was slicked back, and, okay, he had eyeliner on his left eye, but he didn't look like a nutcase. He just looked very…serious. Morose, maybe, like he was trying to creep out the photographer. And weirdly sexy. "You exaggerate everything."

"And look at *this*," Kyle said, flipping to another Post-it note. This time it was a double-page spread of pictures from Spirit Week. One photo was of a bleacher filled with kids, a lot of them with their mouths open, caught in mid-scream, and all of them facing off to the end of the basketball court where the action was—except for one face that was staring into the camera.

Garret Johnson, with the same expression he had in his headshot. Kyle had drawn a circle around him with a highlighter.

"You're so gay!" I told him. "You're obsessed! How did you even spot him?"

"I'm *not* obsessed. I'm *afraid*. This guy's going to be living *in our house*."

"What did you do, cover every inch of this book with a magnifying glass, looking for him?" I started flipping through pages.

He took the book away from me and slammed it shut. "Forget it," he said. "When he soaks you in formaldehyde and eats your liver for breakfast, don't come crying to me."

"I think you protest too much," I told him. "I think you're intrigued." In truth, *I* was a little intrigued. "Now get out. Your two minutes are up."

He took the book with him, which was too bad because I sort of felt like looking at those pictures again. Sometimes I didn't know what to do with myself if I wasn't harassing Kyle or laughing at Sasha or flirting with Jacob. Weird how you can be in a house with so many other people and feel utterly alone.

3. KYLE:
Sexual psychologist,
when I want to be

I'd lied to Judy. I hadn't been emailing my English paper to myself when she'd walked in, because I hadn't written it yet. I'd been checking out a site called mostbeautifulman.com and had switched to email when I'd heard her coming up the stairs.

My paper was supposed to be both *informational* and *organizational*. Why not *informative* and *organized*, I had no idea, but whatever. We could pick our own topic, but we had to make an outline that we turned in with the paper, and both the outline and the paper had to have three different strategically organized points on the topic. Ian and I were in the same English class. The next morning, I called him and asked what he was writing about.

"Bulimia as Fashion Statement," he said.

"That's sick. You're not going to turn into one of those urge-to-purgers, are you?"

"God, no. I can't. I've tried, but all I do is cough. Nothing comes up."

"Good."

"It's terrible for your teeth, anyway. Vomiting, I mean. And it gives you bad breath. No, my paper's on statistical data about supermodel bulimics and how they're practically expected never to digest food if they want to get anywhere in the business."

"Wow. You're taking this assignment seriously."

"What else do I have to do?"

I imagined how calm, how silent his house was. At that moment, sitting in the kitchen, I could hear the living room television, Dexter's drums coming up from the basement, and the thump-thump-thumping of someone (probably Trisha) throwing something (probably a tennis ball) against one of the upstairs walls.

"What are *you* writing about?" Ian asked.

"I have no idea," I said. Then I told him about Garret Johnson's imminent arrival.

Ian didn't know him. "Is he cute?"

"Cute? You haven't seen this guy sitting around the Commons with his sketch pad, drawing people?"

"I live in the bubble that is Ian. Sometimes I get to school and find out my socks don't match. So is he?"

"He's not the kind of guy where *cute* or *not cute* factor into the equation."

"What *does* factor into the equation?"

"He's just...not your average person."

"Well, he doesn't sound boring. He's piqued your interest, at least."

That sounded a little too close to Judy telling me I was intrigued. Suddenly, I wasn't in the mood to talk about Garret Johnson with anyone. I told Ian I had to get started on my paper, which was due in the morning, and got off the phone.

Upstairs, lying on my bed with a legal pad in front of me, I wrote:

AN INFORMATIONAL AND ORGANIZATIONAL ESSAY
ON GARRET JOHNSON

1. TOPIC PARAGRAPH/CONTROLLING IDEA:
GARRET JOHNSON IS A DANGEROUS FREAK
   A. TAKE ONE LOOK AT HIM
   B. TRY TALKING TO HIM
   C. ASK ANYBODY

I crumpled this up, of course, and finally settled on writing about the construction of an acoustic guitar.

Were Judy and Ian right? Was I intrigued? Intrigued was a normal thing to be, wasn't it? Hell, yes, I was intrigued—and with good reason.

It wasn't just that people avoided Garret, and it wasn't just that he'd made that creepy reference to a strangling device in history class. Ferris Coover, who hated his own first name and insisted on being called "Coover" or "the Coove" (nobody opted for "the Coove"), had warned me, months ago during shop class, that Garret was dangerous.

"Dangerous how?" I'd asked. We'd both been assigned the tedious task of sorting through a box of screws. Specifically, we were separating the Phillips heads from the flat heads. "You got some problem with him?"

"No more than I have with any other source of darkness."

I should tell you a little about Ferris Coover—not that I want you thinking Milton High is up to its neck in weirdos (every school has freaks and weirdos, right?), but at Milton, Coover was maybe the *most* weird of them all. Or at least, he *showed* it the most, and almost seemed proud of it. He was a short, stocky kid who sported an old-fashioned flattop and almost always wore striped T-shirts. His freckled, mean-looking face was made even meaner by him scowling all the time. Working against this, his voice was pinched and phlegmy. When he sat during class listening to the teacher, when he ate his lunch in the cafeteria, even when he walked down the halls, his squared-off hands rested in fists. He talked about "the dark side" like he was Obi-Wan Kenobi; "the dark side," he said, surrounded us at any given moment, and you had to keep your guard up against it. He'd been working since the seventh grade on a novel called *And Evil Fell Upon Them*. Currently, he was on spiral-bound, handwritten volume number seven.

There were other dangerous kids at our school, he told me that day, other "sources of darkness," and he listed them as we stood there organizing screws. The names left my head almost as quickly as he said them, except for Garret's.

Nobody took Coover seriously (how could you?). But I couldn't resist wanting to pump him for a little more information, now that I knew Garret was coming to stay with us.

At the end of gym class two days later, I stole a quick glance at Garret, who was sitting on a bench tying his black leather high-tops. In general, I tried not to have roaming eyes too much in the locker room, when all the guys were changing clothes. I *wanted* to, of course, but it wasn't exactly the ideal time to throw a boner when you were coming out of the shower or changing your clothes, so I kept my head down mostly and thought about dead puppies and deformities, stuff like that. But I was becoming a little...preoccupied, let's say...with Garret. His black hair was wet and scattered over his forehead. He was focused on his shoes but at the same time seemed to be taking it all in.

Coover's locker was three down from mine. Buttoning my shirt, I walked over to him and whispered, "What did you mean that day in shop, when you told me Garret was 'dangerous'?"

"Look it up in the dictionary," Coover said.

"I'm serious. He's going to be living in my house for a month."

"Really? You're going to let that kind of evil under your own roof?"

I felt like I was in a scene from his novel. "What did you mean by 'dangerous'?" I hissed.

Coover sighed. He closed his locker and punched the lock shut, then turned to face me full-on. "I shouldn't be telling you this. It's not the kind of information that can just be tossed around lightly." Another sigh. A lowering of that phlegmy voice. "The fact is, he's a vampire."

I couldn't help myself; I started laughing.

"Laugh if you must," Coover said.

I took a quick glance at Garret and was startled to see him looking right at me. There was no way he could have heard us from all the way across the room — but still, it was a little creepy. When I'd stopped laughing, I asked, "What the hell are you talking about?"

"You heard me," Coover said, and started walking away.

"Hey!" I said. But just then the bell rang, and because there were about fifty kids in my gym class, the place turned into Grand Central, and a second later Coover was lost in the shuffle.

I had Spanish after that. We had to write five original compound sentences and read them aloud to the class. I wrote out six, and the one I didn't read aloud was *En tres dias, tendré un vampiro en mi casa, y este no está bueno.*

Sometimes I wondered if Coover might be gay, only because he never dated girls, was so closed-off from other people, and looked like someone who would be an outsider for his entire life. I thought about that. Pretty unflattering attributes, besides the never-dated-girls part, and what did that say about what I thought of gay people? What did it say about what I thought of *myself*? The difference, in my case, was that I was more or less comfortable with who I was and had told my family and a handful of friends. Maybe it was gay guys who hadn't quite figured out they were gay yet, or who suspected it and were freaked out, who were the closed-off outsider loonies.

And if it were theoretically possible that Coover's oddness was the product of his *maybe* being gay...then the same theory could be applied to Garret Johnson.

I was a regular sexual psychologist when I wanted to be.

But here's a relevant piece of information: I, Kyle Renneker, was more than just a gay kid who'd figured things out enough to accept himself and tell his family and quite a few of his friends what the deal was. I was more than just *out*. I was a full-fledged, card-carrying, knows-the-secret-handshake homosexual. When Dad had asked me if I'd *explored* the issue— meaning, had I fooled around with another guy—I'd shaken my head *no* emphatically, and it was true at the time.

It wasn't true anymore.

So I was sitting at Ashley Wells's house one evening last year with five other kids, all of us students of Mr. Cannadera, the humanities teacher who was about to retire. He'd been nice enough, and we all liked him, so we were trying to come up with some sort of lunchtime, end-of-your-glorious-career party we could throw for him on the Commons. We might as well have been plotting world domination. Could we simply decide who was bringing the cake, who was bringing the plastic forks, who was blowing up the balloons? No—mainly because Ashley Wells has "a Type-A, controlling personality," as Dad would say. I kid you not, we got there at seven, and at nine-thirty she cocked her head to one side and said, "Maybe we should use parliamentary procedure to make sure this is worked out fairly."

"Gotta go," a girl at the end of the couch blurted out.

"Me, too," said another.

I jumped up from my chair. "Can I use your phone? I need to call my brother for a ride."

"No, you don't," a voice said. I looked over, and there was blue-eyed Brent Hartley staring at me with a little smile bending up one corner of his mouth. Of course, I'd been checking him out; he had tennis player's legs and creamy skin and was cute enough to have his own series (*Brent Hartley* starring in *MILTON PEAK*). But we'd never really hung out before and I'd never seen him look twice at me. He was a *senior*, for God's sake—why *would* he ever look my way?

"I don't?" I asked him.

He shrugged. "I'll give you a ride. You live off Filmont, right? It's on the way for me."

"How do you know where I live?"

"Because I know your brother Dexter. Well, sort of. We've had a couple of classes together."

I nodded and tried to look cool, but the fact was, I was suddenly so nervous that my whole head was rattling, and I knew Brent could probably see it.

"What about all this stuff we haven't decided on yet?" Ashley asked in a whiny tone, holding up her BlackBerry.

Still looking at me, without letting the smile slip away from his lips, Brent said, "Just decide everything for us, Ashley. Email us what to do. We trust your leadership." He rolled his eyes so that only I could see and asked, "Ready to go?"

Fast-forward. We were in his car, driving toward town and talking. Ashley lived about twenty minutes out, so there was plenty of time to chat on the way back. We talked about Milton, the school; Milton, the town; Milton, the author of *Paradise Lost* (just kidding on that last one). We talked about how Brent was going off to U.Va. in August. And we talked about how weird it was that we were two years apart but still knew a lot of the same kids at school.

"Oh!" he said, like he'd almost forgotten something important, "you want to see a wild sight?"

Who was I to say no to a wild sight? "Sure."

He turned onto a side road, into one of the newer neighborhoods still under construction on the edge of town, and suddenly it was like we'd left civilization behind. "Look at that," he said, slowing down to a stop and pointing through the windshield.

In the glow of the headlights, I saw a giant, round clearing—a spot where they were going to build a McMansion—cut into the orange clay. The clearing was almost a perfect circle and had grooves in it from the teeth marks of a bulldozer that was parked nearby.

"Doesn't it look like a spot where a UFO would land? Or has already landed?" Brent asked.

"I guess," I said. "Yeah. It's pretty cool."

"Anyway," he said, driving right out into the clay, "if we know a lot of the same people, it's weird we haven't hung out before." We reached the center of the circle and he stopped again. This time, he shut off the headlights and the engine. "You know, Tonya Fields is a good friend of mine."

"Really?" Tonya Fields was a good friend of mine, too. So good a friend, in fact, that I'd come out to her two weeks before. "Tonya's great," I said.

"The best. She's so funny when she just blurts out anything."

"Yeah," I said, still not sure where this was going.

"So, can I..." Brent glanced at himself in the rearview mirror and ran his hands through his hair. "...can I ask you something?"

"Sure." My heart was pounding. I swallowed, and it sounded like someone's foot coming down on an empty milk jug.

"You're gay, right? I mean, if you're not, my bad. Forget I said anything. It's just that Tonya told me you were—only because she knew I'd be fine with it. Because I...well, you know...she just thought I'd be interested in knowing."

I stared out at the dark orange field surrounding us, and my heart was in my ears now, *whump, whump, whump,* and I had this totally moronic sequence of thoughts: *Something gay is about to happen here. This spot will forevermore be the place where you had your first gay encounter. People will live here one day, in a nice big house, and never know they're living on a sacred ground of gayness.*

Up to this point, I'd only ever kissed one person, and that was Ian. It wasn't a romantic kiss; it was an experiment. He'd come out, I'd come out, we were sitting around his room one afternoon talking about how it would be, kissing another guy, and then we were like, why not? So we gave it a shot. I'm not attracted to Ian and I don't think he's attracted to me, so maybe that's why the kiss felt like four pieces of cooked pasta shells sliding together. Anyway, we only did it that one time, so with Brent, I wasn't even really sure I knew *how* to kiss.

"Cool," I told him.

"Really?" he said. "You're cool with this?" He waved his hand a little, indicating the car, the two of us sitting in it, the night sky beyond the windshield.

"Sure."

That was all he needed to hear. He leaned across the space between the bucket seats and kissed me. Suddenly, we were making out—full-fledged. And it did *not* feel like cooked pasta shells. It felt amazing. Neon. And of course I was so hard, I thought I was doing permanent denim-confining damage to myself...but then his hand was there, and he was putting *my* hand on him. And I was loving every bit of it, but all the time I was also thinking that I *couldn't* be this lucky. *Okay, this is as far as it will go.... This is as far as it will go.... THIS, come on, **THIS** has GOT to be as far as it will go.* I stopped wondering how far it would go when we both had our pants and underwear down around our ankles and his head was in my lap. It felt like my dick was being abducted by those aliens he'd mentioned and transported to the planet WARM in the galaxy of WET in the solar system of OH MY GOD BRENT HARTLEY IS GIVING ME A BLOW JOB.

A little while later, after I'd gotten beyond feeling like I might pass out, he taught me to do everything to him that he'd just done to me. That part was incredible, too, but in a different way. His mouth on me felt all about me; my mouth on him felt all about him *and* me (and I didn't do a bad job of it, for my first time out).

Twenty minutes later, we were driving again...and Brent's mood had changed. He almost seemed mad. Or scared. Or both.

"I didn't make you do that," he said, his eyes on the road.

"I know. I wanted to do it."

"You *cannot* tell Dexter."

"My whole family already knows I'm gay."

"You can't tell *any*one what we just did. Understand?"

"Okay," I said. And it really was fine with me—I was just wondering how soon we could do it again. Finally, I asked him that very question.

"I don't know," Brent said, glancing at himself in the rear-view mirror again, this time to rub at one corner of his mouth with his thumb. "Probably never."

"Why?"

"Too risky. It's a small town; half the kids I know are going to U.Va. in the fall. It's not like I won't ever see any of them again.

If they found out, I'd never live it down. You are what people think of you—you know?"

"I won't tell."

"Plus, I've got a girlfriend and I don't want to screw that up."

"You've got a *girlfriend*? But we just..."

"What's that got to do with anything?" he muttered, turning in at my driveway.

So I thanked him for the ride and got out of the car.

And that was it for me and Brent Hartley. We never got together again, and come August, he wasn't even a resident of Milton anymore.

Cue the violins. The camera slowly pans back, and lonely little me becomes smaller and smaller, until finally I'm nothing more than a speck in the bottom corner of the screen.

Not! Okay, so maybe I wasn't thrilled about not seeing him again, and maybe I cried a few times, and got in a really bad mood when we had old Mr. Cannadera's retirement cakefest and Brent didn't even bother showing up, and maybe, just *maybe*, I looked up his number in the phone book and called him and never got past his grouch of a mom, who always said he wasn't "available to talk." But so what? I'd had sex! I'd had *gay* sex! And I wasn't even a senior yet!

After Spanish, I had American History—the other class I shared with Garret Johnson. I rounded the corner in B wing, and there he was, leaning against the wall near the door to the classroom, his thin wisp of a body curling so that one hip was against his schoolbooks and sketchbook and the other was touching the brick. He was staring right at me (an intense look that was half-eyelinered). Keep in mind that, while we'd seen each other a lot over the school year, and had classes that overlapped, we'd never once spoken to each other.

As I was passing him, he said, "You're Kyle Renneker."

"That's me," I said, curt as possible. But then I thought of what Dad had told us about making Garret feel welcome while he stayed with us. I stopped and readjusted my books. "You're Garret Johnson."

"Guilty," he said in that dry, cool voice. "I take it you're a Dylan fan."

How did he know that? I wondered — then I remembered I was wearing my *Highway 61* T-shirt, new but with the image pre-scuffed up, as if I were an old man and had owned it since the sixties. "Dylan's the king."

"Of?"

I said the safest thing that came to mind. "Songwriters."

"I guess you and I are going to be roommates in a few days."

Roommates? I wanted to set the record straight on that one fast. "Well, not really. I think you're going to be staying in the attic."

"The attic," he said. "How appropriate. Amusing, even."

Did I know any other kids who used phrases like *amusing, even*? I didn't. Nor did I know any other kids who were vampires. But that was Coover's craziness, I reminded myself, and it wasn't fair to push it on Garret. I said, "The attic's really cool. Well, I guess it's cool. I haven't seen it since my dad turned it into a game room. He's a real perfectionist, though, so it's probably the nicest room in the house."

"I don't mind staying in the attic," he said, staring right at me. His eyes, I have to admit, were kind of hypnotizing, and I think he knew it. He wasn't grinning, but he wasn't frowning, either. He was watching me watch him...watch me. "Sorry," he said. "I can't help but leer."

I didn't know what *leer* meant. I made a mental note to look it up later.

"My family's kind of huge," I said. "There are nine of us. It can get a little crazy."

"You're a reality show waiting to happen."

"More like some corny rerun from the seventies. *Nine Is Too Many*." I probably shouldn't have said that, since he was about to make us ten.

"Well, truly, the attic suits me quite well."

Truly. Suits me. Quite well. Who *was* this guy?

"What have you been drawing?" I asked, glancing down at his sketch pad.

"People. Their auras, anyway. The way they look inside out, metaphorically speaking."

He didn't offer to show me any of these "auras." I nodded toward my history book. "You read the chapter for today?"

"No," he said, taking his eyes off me finally and glancing into the classroom. "I know all about the Louisiana Purchase, and whatever Ms. Ramble-On has to say about it" (her name was Ms. Ramplin) "really doesn't interest me much. Some mor —" He caught himself there, skipped a beat, and went on: "Some people really do have such a narrow view of history, as if they were born *days* ago. Shall we?"

He gestured toward the classroom door just as the bell rang. I followed him in.

"The whole idea behind the Purchase was gaining access to the Mississippi," Ms. Ramplin was saying. "Once Thomas Jefferson found out the Spanish had ceded Louisiana to the French, he set about acquiring what two things?"

No one responded.

"Well, I'll tell you this much, it wasn't cow eyes and fish mouths. And that's all I see when I look out at your faces. Did anyone even bother to *read* this chapter?"

I was only half paying attention. I was thinking about that remark Garret had made. *Some mor* — What was the end of his phrase going to be? Whatever he'd been going to say, he'd replaced it with *some people.*

I ran through a list of possibilities, given the context of his remark.

Some morally corrupt people...

Some morons...

Some more pie, please?

Or

Some mortals...

I was obsessing. I was being paranoid. My brain had been Cooverized.

As Ms. Ramplin talked about James Monroe and money and constitutional interpretation, I looked behind me and over a couple of rows, to where Garret sat. There he was, looking down at his notebook, where he seemed to be drawing something. As if he could feel my gaze, he lifted his head and his eyes searched the room. I quickly looked away.

Cooverized, I told myself. *You're officially infected with that little runt's wackiness.*

I knew Coover's last class was Driver's Ed. I knew they were done training in the actual cars and were back in the classroom, reviewing traffic laws and watching those gory, wear-your-seat-belt-or-else films. When the bell rang, I bolted out of History and made my way to D wing as fast as I could, so I could catch Coover before he left.

I spotted his flat-topped head and striped shirt as he made his way down the hall. Quick-stepping to catch up with him, I landed a hand on his shoulder.

He spun around, one fist raised up in front of his chest. There was a gold ring on every finger.

No, they weren't rings. He was brandishing a set of brass knuckles.

"That's a good way to get yourself punched," he said, realizing it was me.

"What the hell are those?"

"What do they look like?"

"I mean, what are they *for*?"

"Protection," he said, casting his beady eyes right and left, as if fearing assassins. "Evil forces can swoop down without a second's warning, and you have to be ready. Sometimes you have to attack them *first*. Land the first blow, you know?"

"Listen," I said, a little out of breath from racing to catch up with him, "you were screwing with me earlier, right?"

"I don't *screw* with anyone," he said.

Taken in the literal sense, a greater truth probably had never been spoken. "I mean, when you said that stuff about Garret being a vampire. You're just collecting ideas for your novel, right?"

"It's not a novel anymore."

"No? What's it now, a musical?"

"It's *nonfiction*. It's about what I've observed firsthand of the dark world, and my efforts to put a stop to it. I hope, for your sake, that I don't end up having to write a chapter about *you*."

"You're so wacked," I said, irritated that he wouldn't budge. "Even if something as crazy as that were true—*even if* —how would you know about it?"

"I know," Coover said, readjusting his hand so that the brass knuckles fit more snugly, "because Garret told me himself."

Regardless of *what* Garret was, something about this rang true. Or at least, Coover believed that Garret had said as much. I could see the utter conviction in his eyes.

He sniffed the air, glanced around again, and lowered his voice. "If that guy's going to be living in your house, watch your back," he said. He started to turn away, then paused, looked at me, and added, "And your neck."

4. JUDY:
Who would Jesus bazooka?

Jacob loves me and I know
For the bible tells me so.

atchy, right? Of course, the bible didn't tell me any such thing, but holding that little book made me feel close to him. While some kids gave me friendly nods when they saw it in my hands, others stared at me like at any minute I might speak in tongues, or serve cups of poisoned Kool-Aid. But I didn't care. Sometimes I'd even tilt my head back just a little and look down my nose at them. It was fun feeling superior to everyone around me because I'd found religion—even if I hadn't found it.

Well, actually I had. I found it *boring*.

Only Sasha was in on the secret, and that was a potential mistake because she could be such a blabbermouth. After school on Friday, she was sitting on a concrete bench outside waiting for her mom to pick her up, with her oboe in its giant black case beside her. She was staring off into space, and her expression was so sad, you would have thought her dog had just died. "What's wrong?" I asked, sitting down next to her.

"Nothing!" Her face sprang alive when she saw me. She was all smiles. Honestly, I never knew what was going on in her head. "So how's it going with the holy roll-up?"

"I think you mean holy *roller*. And it's fine," I said. "Well, not fine." I spelled out what had happened at the last bible study, and my stalemate with Tina. "You should see this girl. She's so pretty, you just want to slap her."

"Do you think she's after Jacob?"

"I don't know. I don't see how *he* could like *her*, though. She's the biggest phony; everything she says sounds so...insincere."

"Phony? So you think *she's* faking it, too?"

Had Sasha just compared me to Tina? I said, "I don't mean *that*. What *I'm* doing is totally different. I'm faking being saved because I *like* someone. That's a *good* thing. Tina probably *is* saved—hallelujah for her—but she's faking her whole existence. She's one of those beautiful, plastic people who always have a little act going on. She's like...Barbie! That's what she is: a life-sized Barbie doll."

The expression on Sasha's face changed yet again. Her eyes darted past my shoulder and her mouth hung open for a moment. Then she said, "Quick, what's your favorite prayer?"

"Huh? Earth to Sasha, are you even listening to what I've been saying? I want to blow that girl up with a bazooka!"

"*Prayer,*" Sasha said, bugging her eyes out at me. "What's your favorite *prayer*?"

I thought she'd gone mental. But after a second I looked behind me, and there stood Jacob, dressed in jeans and his football jersey, his backpack slung over one shoulder. Damn! How long had he been standing there?

"Oh!" I said, swinging my head back to Sasha, "that walk-through-the-valley-of-death one, for sure! Can't remember what it's called." I turned back around to face Jacob. "Hi!"

"Hi," he said.

His expression was the polar opposite of Sasha's. That is, it didn't jump around like it belonged to someone with multiple personalities. It was handsome and level and calm, very sexy. Like Jesus's, if Jesus had short hair and no beard.

"It's called the Twenty-third Psalm," he said.

"The twenty-third what?"

"Psalm. That prayer you were just saying is your favorite."

I felt my face flush. "Right," I said, "the twenty-*third* one. I always confuse it with the twenty-fourth. Have you met Sasha? Sasha, this is Jacob. Jacob, Sasha."

"Hi!" Sasha said with the enthusiasm of a lady on an infomercial. "I've heard a lot about you!"

"Really?" Jacob asked.

"Oh, yeah! If Judy isn't talking about God and the bible, she's talking about you."

Shut up, Sasha, I thought.

"I mean it. If she isn't saying a prayer, she's saying the name 'Jacob.'"

"Shut up, Sasha," I said aloud, and forced a little laugh behind it. "That's so not true."

"Judy's the most religious person I know."

I wanted to stomp on her foot. I wanted to hit her over the head with her oboe. "So what's up?" I asked Jacob, fingering the edges of the bible on top of my schoolbooks.

"I wanted to let you know, we're not having study group tomorrow night."

"Oh. Why not?"

"I just have so much schoolwork. I have this huge paper due in humanities, and I haven't even started it yet. I think I need the extra time to work on it."

I smelled a rat. He'd come over to tell me something else, I thought, and was making up this lie on the spot because he'd overheard what I'd said about Tina. Maybe he even *liked* Tina—more than in just that way he was supposed to like all God's creatures—and he was angry with me now.

But, wait. If he was still intending to have his study, could he lie to me? I mean, was that allowed? Lying was a sin (just like swearing and threatening to...bazooka people). I stared into his eyes and asked, "So you're saying there isn't going to be a bible study at your house tomorrow?"

"Right," he said, looking down at his sneakers.

"Okay," I said. "Well, maybe I could come over anyway and help you with your paper. English is my best subject."

"He said it was for humanities, not English," Sasha said.

I glared at her, and she drew her lips together. "What I mean," I said, "is that I'm really good at writing papers, so I could help you, if you want."

"No, thanks," Jacob said. He slid his hands into the pockets of his jeans and shrugged, taking a step backward. "I just wanted to let you know."

"All right," I said. "I'll take the night off, too, I guess."

"Sounds good," he said, still backing up. "Well, see you later." He gave a little wave, turned around, and walked away.

"Wow. Did he just blow you off?" Sasha asked.

"Shut it," I said, and got up from the bench.

That night I was on salad duty. It sounds like nothing, but believe me, when you have to make salad for nine people—nine *picky* people—it's a major ordeal. There couldn't be just one giant bowl that everyone took from. Oh, no. Dawn was allergic to sunflower seeds. Suzie wanted a whole bowl of sunflower seeds with a little bit of lettuce on top. Trisha couldn't have tomatoes because of *her* allergies, and Kyle hated carrots. Both Tommy and Mom didn't like raw onions. Dad only wanted the *hearts* of the lettuce heads (which weren't hearts at all but those bitter stems in the middle). And could any three of them like the same kind of dressing? Forget it. Blue cheese, Thousand

Island, ranch, honey mustard, vinaigrette, Russian, some disgusting thing called *Cheesy Cheese* that Dexter was crazy about—all of them had to be carried out to the table.

I was setting the bowls out according to who sat where (assigned seats, you know) when Kyle came into the dining room.

"Did you hear there was a contest?" I asked him before he could say anything.

"What contest?"

"To see which one of us wasn't homosexual. I won."

"Listen." He moved up beside me and lowered his voice. "Do you know what Ferris Coover told me today?"

"Coover? What are you doing talking to *that* creep?"

"He's in my gym class. He told me that Garret Johnson claims to be a vampire."

I stopped what I was doing and just stared at him, a salad bowl in each hand. "I've got the lowdown on Coover, and there's no reason to pay attention to a word he says. But listen, I am not in the mood to go to Kyle Land right now, okay? I'm not really up for Isn't-Bob-Dylan-Hot? or Could-I-Be-Any-Gayer? I've got stuff on my mind. *Real* stuff. So unless you want to wear a salad, clam up and clear out."

"What 'lowdown' do you have on Coover?"

I huffed and rolled my eyes. "He was in my bible study for two weeks before Jacob had to ask him to leave. The guy's bonkers. He was talking seriously about taking steps to *eradicate* the forces of evil from Milton High. As in, one by one, seek them out, attack them, *kill* them. And we basically said, 'Um, see you later?' He told us we were all 'self-deluded fools' and stormed out."

"Does he read the bible?"

"He probably *smokes* the bible. Why don't you ask him, if he's your best friend now?"

"He's not," Kyle said. He was staring at all the bottles of salad dressing and seemed distracted by something for a moment. Then he asked, "How can you be all religious and still be such a monster?"

"History is filled with religious monsters. So do you feel like wearing a salad, or not?"

I lifted a bowl into the air between us like I meant to throw it. He left the dining room.

Dinner was the usual blab fest, but I didn't say a word to anyone. I thought maybe Kyle would bring up his vampire news and almost hoped he would, because it would have made him sound like an idiot. It would have lightened my mood to hear the others laughing at him. But he didn't mention it. Dawn was wearing a baseball hat made out of tinfoil, and Tommy asked her if she was picking up satellite signals. Mom asked Dexter if he'd given any more thought to changing his mind about college in August, and Dexter said no. Dad launched into one of his glorious, sarcastic speeches about how a career as a sporting goods clerk would surely bring Dexter the Nobel Prize one day, and Dexter said he didn't *want* a Nobel Prize and that, once he turned eighteen, he wouldn't have to deal with this "family oppression." Then Trisha asked what *oppression* was, and Dexter told her it was when you didn't want to go to college and your parents forced you to at gunpoint. That really set Mom off. I tried my best to tune them all out.

As soon as the meal was over, I retreated to my room and called Jacob. But how did I want to sound? Miffed? No. Eager? Probably not. Best, I thought, just to sound...curious.

"Hello?"

"Hi, this is Judy. Judy Renneker. Is Jacob around?"

"Jacob! It's for you!" Mr. Lindsey yelled without even lowering the phone. His voice pierced my eardrum.

A few moments later, Jacob got on the line, and Mr. Lindsey hung up.

"Hi, it's Judy."

"Oh—hi, Judy."

"What are you up to?"

"Homework. Finally getting started on this humanities paper. I'm doing it on the Medici family. Do you know who they were?"

"No." Didn't know, didn't care. "Listen, I was curious. If there's not going to be any bible study tomorrow evening, do you think maybe on Sunday—if you get caught up on your paper—you and I might get together for a little bible study makeup session?" I swear, I nearly said "make-out session." Wouldn't that have been subtle? "I just don't want to get behind on the whole Job thing. You know, all that suffering can pile up pretty fast."

"You could always read it on your own."

That stung. I tried not to let it show in my voice. "I know. But you always shed so much light on what we read. And, listen, if you're not a good typist, you can just write your paper out by hand and I'll type it when I'm over there. Or you can come over to my place. We could hang out in my room. Whatever's good for you." I sounded more than curious and worse than eager. I sounded desperate.

"I think I'll just work here, alone," he said. "But thanks."

"Oh, well, okay. Good luck with your work, then. You know, Godspeed and all."

We said goodnight and hung up, and I thought, *What kind of loser sits at home on a Friday night doing homework?* But my very next thought was, *What kind of loser sits at home on a Friday night calling up a boy who may not even be interested in her, trying to scrape together a poor excuse for a date?* I wanted to call him back and ask if next week's bible study was still on—just to make sure I was still in the club—but decided I'd already done enough damage for one night.

The hideous voice of Bob Dylan crackled from Kyle's room down the hall. I got off my bed, marched over to his door, and pounded on it.

"What?" he called from the other side.

I tried the knob. It was unlocked. I pushed the door open and there was Kyle in his T-shirt and shorts, standing in front of his full-length closet mirror with his guitar.

"In love with yourself much?" I asked.

"I'm watching my hand," he said. "I'm learning new chords."

"Right. Turn it down," I told him.

"You should listen to this song. It's called 'Slow Train,' and it's about how we should all wise up and accept the second coming of the Lord. It's right up your born-again alley."

"It's going to be right up your unborn-again ass if you don't turn it down," I said. "Or I could get Mom to *make* you turn it down, in which case I'll win."

"Monster," he said, looking at me in the mirror. "Capital *M*." But he reached over and hit the volume button on his stereo, lowering the nasally twang.

The next morning, I couldn't help wondering if I, like that creepy nutcase Coover, had officially been kicked out of bible study. All I'd done was make a mean comment about Tina. That didn't turn me into a crazy girl who wanted to go on some personal crusade, eradicating evil; it just made me a sensible person who wanted to rid the world of phony, plastic girls who tried to steal would-be boyfriends away from normal people. Nothing so wrong with that, right?

I asked myself:

Should I just call Jacob back and ask him outright if I'm still in the club?

I asked myself:

What would Jesus do?

I did what I'd never done before: I flipped open the bible to the New Testament, landed my finger on one of the Jesus-speak passages in red ink, and read, "Take heed therefore how ye hear: for whosoever hath, to him shall be given; and whosoever hath not, from him shall be taken even that which he seemeth to have."

Thanks, Jesus. Big help.

I closed the book.

Mom had us working double-time that day to get the house ready for Garret Johnson. You would have thought some Hollywood celebrity was about to arrive. Tommy edged the sidewalk and driveway, and Dexter trimmed the hedges. Kyle mowed the lawn, following the power mower like it was a Great Dane yanking him around. Inside, Dawn vacuumed, Suzie dusted, and Trisha had the lame task of "righting" the pictures on the walls and arranging the knickknacks on the mantel and coffee table (oh, to be the youngest and get the nothing jobs!). I, on the other hand, had to clean the entire finished portion of the attic—the quarters for our celebrity guest. There was plaster dust all over the place from where Dad had sanded the walls before the last coat of paint. He was up there with me, finishing the wiring on the wide-screen TV, while I cleaned.

"I don't get it," I complained as I swept the floor. "What do we care what this guy thinks of how clean our house is? We're the ones putting him up for a month."

"We want him to feel comfortable, that's all."

"What's not to be comfortable with? It's a house. It has walls and a roof."

Dad was on his hands and knees behind the TV screen. He lifted his head over the top of it like a hand puppet and said, "As you know, we're a large family, and things can get quite hectic around here. But we're not trashy, Judy, and we don't want to give off that impression."

I dragged a damp cloth over the air hockey table and the blinking Galaga machine. I put fresh sheets on the single bed between the two dormer windows. An annoying little song ran through my head: *Jacob hates me and I know...*

Just after four P.M., a dark green Buick turned into the driveway.

"They're here!" Mom called from the living room.

We all gathered in the foyer, slumping like a reception line deprived of protein. "I have to *pee*," Trisha said, but Mom shushed her. The doorbell rang. Mom opened the door and there stood Mr. and Mrs. Johnson, with Garret leaning to one side behind them, wearing a long black leather coat, even though it was mid-May in Virginia—not exactly a temperature that lent itself to leather (unless you were a horse, or a cow). No eyeliner today, I noticed. He had a backpack on his shoulders and two suitcases at his feet, and he was holding a large sketch portfolio.

"Welcome," Mom said enthusiastically, sweeping her arm

into the house. You would have thought we were selling the place and they were prospective buyers.

"Thank yoouuu," Mrs. Johnson said in a thick Southern drawl. "Oh, you have a *lovely* home!" She stepped inside, all smiles, followed by Mr. Johnson, who was a large, dark-haired man with a mustache that might have been drawn on with Mom's Sharpie.

Was our home lovely? I'd never noticed. It was big, I knew that much, but like an ocean liner bound for chaos.

Garret followed his parents into the foyer.

"Dexter, Tommy, help him with those," Mom said, motioning toward the suitcases.

They took the suitcases from him, and he actually smiled (the first time I'd ever seen him smile) and said, "Very kind of you," and then turned toward our parents, extending a hand. "And it's very kind of you to take me in like this, Mr. and Mrs. Renneker."

"We're glad to do it," Dad told him.

"Honestly," Garret emphasized, his smile broadening to show teeth. "It's the nicest thing I can imagine someone doing for me."

Oh, brother, I thought. *Laying it on a little thick, aren't you?* He certainly didn't seem like the solemn-faced loner I saw at school. He met all nine of us in turn, and shook our hands, and said, "My pleasure," and "How are you?" and, when shaking Kyle's hand, "Nice to see you again."

From the look on Kyle's face, you'd have thought he'd just won a new iPhone. Where had all that fear-of-having-the-vampire-freak-in-our-house worry gone, all of a sudden?

I was over all of them.

Mom offered the Johnsons coffee and Garret a Coke. She led them into the living room, just as Trisha announced again that she had to pee and ran off for the bathroom.

"Gotta go read the bible," I said, turning toward the staircase.

"You have Jesus Club tonight?" Tommy asked.

"No—I mean, yes, I have bible study," I lied, quickly rethinking my options. "I just don't have any way to get there. Can I borrow your car again?"

"Sorry, Mary Magdalene. I need it. I have a date."

I turned to Dexter. "Can I borrow yours? Please?"

Dexter frowned, but said, "If you wash it tomorrow."

"I'll do it," I said. "I promise." Then I bounded up the stairs, like I couldn't wait to get my nose back into the bible.

Again, I asked myself, *What would Jesus do?*

I didn't bother to flip through the book and point with my finger this time. I thought, *Jesus would drive Dexter's car right over to Jacob's house and see if that bitch's yellow convertible is parked out front.*

Dexter's Mustang was newer than Tommy's Volkswagen, but it was in rattier shape. The radio didn't even work. I didn't care, though; I was on a mission. If Tina was there, she was there, and there was nothing I could do to change that. If she wasn't, hoo-ray for me (and hooray for her tires, which I wouldn't have to slash). I just wanted to *know*.

I steered with one hand and rested the other on the bible in my lap, as if it were a good luck charm or some ancient artifact that granted wishes. *No yellow convertible, no yellow convertible,* I thought over and over again.

But when I turned left at the dead refrigerator and pulled up in front of Jacob's car, what did I see?

The yellow convertible. Shining in the moonlight, *glowing,* even. The vanity plates read FUNNGURL17.

I wasn't being serious when I said I was going to slash her tires. I didn't have anything to slash them with. But I gave real thought to ramming her back bumper. Dexter's Mustang was already banged up; he might not notice or even care about a few more dents. They'd hear the noise in the Lindsey house, though. They'd look out the front windows and see me.

Suddenly, I was nervous about being seen, period, so I hit the gas and flew past the house.

That fake, conniving slut. She'd probably made up stories about how phony I was, or trashed me for that stupid JESUS IS COMING. LOOK BUSY T-shirt. It had probably been *her* idea that Jacob lie to me about how there was no bible study tonight.

That was the only way Jacob *would* lie, I decided. He was too good-hearted to do it otherwise.

I followed Compton Street for another couple of blocks, then finally turned around. When I was passing the house for the second time, it dawned on me: Maybe he hadn't lied at all. Maybe there *wasn't* a bible study tonight. I mean, obviously there wasn't a *regular* bible study. Tina's car was the only one parked in front of the house that didn't belong to the Lindseys.

Maybe they were having a date.

I wished all the curses of Job on both of them, and floored it.

I was ugly, I decided on the way home. And too short. My hair was the color of straw and my cheeks were pudgy. Who still had baby fat at sixteen? Me. No wonder Jacob didn't want to date me. By the time I pulled into the driveway, though, I'd lifted the curse on Jacob and only wished it on Tina. Jacob, I'd decided, was under her spell and would eventually come to his senses. I would go on a diet, buy shoes with higher heels, maybe even dye my hair some fancy shade of red.

"Is that you, Judy?" Dad called from the living room.

I stuck my head in, and there they all were (except for Garret), sitting around the television: Mom, Dad, and Dexter on the couch, Tommy and Kyle in the recliners, Dawn, Suzie, and Trisha sprawled out on the floor. Every night in our house looked like a convention at a civic center.

"Come watch this with us," Mom said. "It's a video of you and Kyle on your second birthday."

"You've got cake on your face!" Dawn nearly shouted.

"Look at Tommy's hair!" Suzie said. "He looks like a girl."

"No, I don't. It was just longer than it is now."

"How come I'm not in this movie?" Trisha asked. She was on her stomach, her chin resting on her hands, her legs seesawing back and forth.

"You weren't born yet, Squirt," Dexter told her. "You didn't exist."

"What's *exist*?"

"It means the sperm hadn't penetrated the egg yet."

"Dexter! Really, now," Mom said.

Trisha, of course, immediately asked what a *sperm* was.

Dad cleared his throat. "It's part of what you need to make a baby, but we'll talk about that later. *Much* later."

I looked at the TV screen. Kyle, dressed in short pants and a Teletubbies T-shirt, was running circles around our living room, holding a big stuffed dalmatian in both hands. Dad, in dark horn-rimmed glasses (he wore wire-frames now), was chasing him. The camera was jiggling all over the place. It swung to one side and showed Dexter licking a birthday candle, then swung the other way, and there I was with icing all over my mouth. I looked like a baby pig in a dress.

"I've got stuff to do," I said.

"Well, don't bother Garret," Dad told me.

"Right," I said. Like I'd want to.

"He's upstairs, said he wants some settling-in time."

I went into the kitchen, bypassed the cookies, got a carrot from the fridge, and munched on it on my way up to my bedroom.

Jesus stared at me from over my dresser. *A lot of good you did me*, I thought, looking at the picture. I tossed the bible onto the nightstand and flopped down on the bed, staring at the ceiling.

Then I heard a crash—something glass shattering overhead.

Don't bother Garret.

It was my house, wasn't it? He'd just gotten here and he was already smashing the place up? I got off the bed, went out into the hall, and climbed the stairs to the attic door.

There was a long pause after I knocked. Then a voice said, "Who is it?"

One of the bona fide residents, I thought. "It's Judy. Can I come in?"

"Um...sure."

A few seconds later, the door opened, and Garret looked me up and down, his eyes settling on the carrot. "What's up, doc?"

The eyeliner was back, I noticed. He was dressed in a pair of ratty jeans and a black T-shirt with a collar that looked deliberately ripped. The attic glowed red behind him.

"You're renovating?"

"Sorry," he said, brushing his hair away from his eyes. "I dropped a lightbulb. Do you know if there's a broom and a dustpan around somewhere?"

There was. I'd been using them just that morning. I walked past him into the game room. Every light—even the one in the bathroom—had been replaced with a red bulb. The place looked like a haunted house. Music was leaking out of a laptop in the corner, some girly-sounding guy making soup out of his words. "What is this you're listening to?"

"The Smiths," he said. "Know them?"

"Not biblically." I stepped over to the closet and took the broom and dustpan from their spot next to the rolls of Christmas wrapping paper and stacks of Dad's *Psychology Quarterly* magazines. With the carrot lodged in my mouth, I handed them to him.

"Thanks," he said.

I watched him bend down and sweep up the mess he'd made in the middle of the floor. He dumped the glass and the metal tip of the smashed lightbulb into the bathroom trash can.

"Do you always travel with your own lighting?" I asked.

"Red is the color of my mood," he said without looking at me. "Its hue evens me out."

Right. I sat down on a chair near the air hockey machine. "So how do you like the new digs?"

"They're great," he said. "Maybe not as baroque as I'd like, but nice."

He was freakishly skinny. His legs looked like twigs and his long arms were pale and thin, like pipe cleaners. He replaced the broom and dustpan in the closet, then walked over to his suitcase, which he was still unpacking. Nearly all of the clothes he pulled out of it were black—his T-shirts, his socks, even his underwear, which he didn't seem at all embarrassed about my seeing as he transferred them from the suitcase to the dresser beneath the brand-new dartboard.

"Why all the black?" I asked around the carrot. "Does that reflect your mood, too?"

"Actually, red is the color of my mood, and black is the color of my aura. What color is *your* aura?"

It's going to be a long month, I thought. "I don't think I've ever noticed. Or cared. So how does it feel, joining the cast of *A Thousand Clowns*?"

"Strange," he said, refolding a T-shirt. "I mean, everyone's nice."

"You were quiet at dinner." In fact, he'd also been ultra-polite. He'd *thank you'd* everyone and even *sirred* and *ma'amed* Dad and Mom, till they'd told him he didn't have to do that.

"It wasn't exactly easy to get a word in edgewise," he told me.

"Very Renneker. So how come you're Captain Manners around my parents? You don't have to be. Trisha usually burps whatever she has to say."

"I find manners can open doors. Or keep them closed."

I didn't know what that meant, but didn't ask.

"It's odd being around so many people," he said. "For me, anyway. I'm someone who appreciates solitude."

That sounded like an invitation for me to leave. "Well, you've come to the wrong place. Around here, you're bumping into one person and tripping over another one everywhere you go. It's just the way it is."

He was done unpacking. He closed the suitcase and put it

beside the bed. Then he sat down on the mattress and looked at me. "Don't finish that carrot."

I stopped chewing. "Huh?"

"I want to draw you with it sticking out of your mouth like that. Like a cigar."

Whoa. Was that some sort of sick phallic reference he'd just made? "You want to *draw* me?"

"May I?" He was already digging his sketch pad out of his portfolio case and reaching for a small plastic box. He opened the box and took out a piece of charcoal. "I work fast. It's the only way to truly capture a person's aura."

"*Girlfriend in a coma, I know, I know, it's serious,*" the singer moaned. Could we be listening to a creepier song?

Suddenly, I felt a little uncomfortable.

"No," I told him.

He was holding the charcoal, about to start making lines on the sketch pad balanced in his lap. When he looked up, he seemed confused. Maybe even a little miffed. "No?"

"I don't feel like it," I said. "Besides, you can't just go around drawing everybody you want to."

"Sure I can. I do it all the time."

"Well, you can't draw me." I wasn't sure why I was telling him no. I was in a bad mood, but I guess, also, I didn't want him thinking he had some sort of control over me. He was one of those people who, when he looked at you, held his eye contact about one second too long, and didn't blink enough. He seemed to *enjoy* making people uncomfortable. I felt like turning the tables a little. "You should ask my brother Kyle if you can draw *him*. I'm sure he'd love it."

"Would he?" Garret dropped the charcoal back into the box and closed the lid. He set the sketch pad on the bed next to him, then reclined, facing me, until his shoulders were propped against the wall and his skinny legs were draped over the edge of the mattress.

"He's gay, you know. He's *out* and *proud*."

"And gay people like to be drawn more than straight people do?"

"He'd like to be drawn by *you*, is what I'm saying. He has the hots for you." I wasn't sure if this was actually true or not, but I didn't care. I was going for the shock value.

But it didn't seem to faze Garret one bit. In fact, he even nodded his head a little, as if people announced that their gay brothers had crushes on him every day. *Oh my God,* I thought, *maybe he is gay.* I'd made that stupid comment to Kyle about how the eyeliner might make Garret half a drag queen, and half gay, but I hadn't even been half serious when I'd said it.

"Do *you*?" he asked.

I nearly spit out the last inch of carrot. "Do I what?"

"Have the hots for me?"

I couldn't believe how blunt he was. What was his deal, anyway? Did he swing toward girls or boys?

"*Do you think I'm hot?*" he rephrased, articulating his words as if I were a foreigner.

Maybe he was bisexual. He was staring at me dead-on, waiting for an answer. I guess I sort of *did* think he was hot, in a freak-of-nature kind of way. And if he truly was bi, that meant Kyle had as much a chance with him as I did. I actually didn't even *want* a chance with him; I wanted my chance with Jacob. But if Kyle wanted him and Kyle had a shot...and *I* had a shot...

Well, I wasn't about to toss *that* one away.

"You're hot enough," I told Garret.

"Enough?" He laughed—I'd never heard him laugh before; there was a lot of breath in it, as if he were being squeezed. It was kind of cute, in a way. "Enough for *what*?"

I didn't answer this. I gave him what I hoped was something between a sneer and a smile and said, "I've heard some things about you, you know."

He pushed his back away from the wall, curled slowly forward, and rested his elbows on his knees, his long hands draped together. "I've heard some things about you, too."

"Like what?"

"I heard you're a born-again."

I wondered if his thinking that might hurt my chances with him (or even increase them?). "So? Lots of people are religious."

"Well..." he said, as if deciding where he wanted the conversation to go next. "Tell me more about Kyle. And about you. You two are Gemini?"

"Leo," I said. "Not that I believe in that stuff."

"I mean, you're twins."

"Unfortunately. Smack in the middle of the brood. With so many people, there's always *some* drama going on."

He rattled off all seven of our names as if he were being quizzed, and he nailed every one of them except for "Tom."

"He goes by Tommy. *His* big drama was getting caught with a joint senior year, but I think being grounded for a whole month was enough to put him off drugs forever."

An electronic bat-chirping noise rose above the music.

He pulled a cell phone out of his backpack. "Sorry," he said, "I *must* take this." Turning away from me, he opened the phone and said, "Hello?"

He didn't make any effort to lower his voice, so I didn't make any effort *not* to listen in.

"Yes, I'm here. . . . Yes, it's fine. They're nice, for mortals. Blood type? Does it matter?" He glanced over at me. "What blood type are you?"

"I don't know. O-positive, I think."

"You should *always* know your blood type," he said. Then, into the phone, "She thinks she's O-positive. Well, I could only guess, but maybe they're *all* O-positive. It's AB-negative that upsets my stomach. Don't worry; I won't starve. There's always regular food, you know. All right. All right. I've got to go—bye."

He hung up and put the phone away. "So, where were we?"

"Um, what the hell was *that* all about?"

"Nothing."

"Who *was* that? And what did you mean, 'They're nice, for mortals'?"

"That was Helena. She's sort of my...trainer."

Blood types. Hunger. "Your *vampire* trainer?"

"It's complicated. Don't worry about it," he said, giving me the thinnest of smiles.

He was beyond weird, I decided. He was playing with me. And he was getting cuter by the minute. The music ended and the room—still glowing red—went quiet. I thought about how different Jacob was from Garret, and how my heart was with Jacob even though my mind, at the moment, was with Garret. I thought about that bitch, Tina. She was pretty and I was fat. She was a Barbie doll and I was a...marshmallow.

As if he could read my thoughts and wanted to counteract them, Garret said, "You're a pretty girl. Do you know that?"

I glanced around, trying to think of something to say that would keep us talking. Finally, I said, "You know, all the other kids are in an uproar over you staying in the game room. They've been waiting for Dad to finish this place for *months*. Kyle, especially. I mean, he's got a crush on you and all, but he's really pissed about you being up here."

"It's a cool room," Garret said. "I'd be pissed, too. But they can come up and play whenever they want."

"Nope. Dad was specific: We can only come up if you invite us."

"That didn't seem to slow you down any."

"I'm my own boss," I said. My eyes landed on the Ms. Pac-Man game. "Do you know how to play that one?"

"Sure. It's a great game."

"Maybe you could teach me."

"I'd be happy to," he said. Then he leaned forward again, his elbows resting on his knees, and added, "*If* I can draw you."

5. K Y L E :
The Great Unspoken Act

I've had a lot of crushes, and I find a lot of people hot. I'm basically the horniest person on Earth—which isn't necessarily an exaggeration, because there's no way to prove anybody is hornier than me (what are you going to do, poll the whole planet?), and I'm happy to assume the title.

What I *wasn't* happy about was having a crush on someone I didn't necessarily like.

Of course, it had happened before. In school, for instance, just because a guy was a bully or a jerk, that didn't change the fact that he was awesome looking. It *should* have. If there was any justice in the world, behaving like a bully or a jerk wouldn't just change the way other people saw you; it would make you grow an elbow out of your forehead or an extra ear on your chin. It would make you gross. But if a guy made fun of me in gym for not being the best football catcher, or tried to trip me in the hallway for no reason at all (not that this was a daily occurrence or anything), and if that guy had a nice butt and muscular arms and a really great-looking face? He got to keep all that stuff, and I was still stuck with him in my mental cast of hotties when it came time to...you know.

It didn't seem fair.

The more I thought of what Coover had told me about Garret, the more I wanted to know. The more I watched Garret, the more I *wanted* to watch him—like at the dinner table his first night in our house, for instance, when he listened to Dad describe what a beta-blocker was and how not only musicians but actors and public speakers were using them now to prevent their brains from making them nervous. Garret nodded his head and said things like, "That's fascinating, Mr. Renneker," while his eyes ticked over to me as I cleared the dishes.

Sunday afternoon, I was in my room with the door locked and the music on low (so Monster wouldn't complain). I was listening to *Blonde on Blonde*, lying on my bed, doing that thing we all do but pretend we don't—funny that it's more awkward talking about *that* than it is talking about actual sex, or maybe it's just less interesting because there's only one party involved. Anyway, I was doing it, and for the first time since I was eleven and had discovered the joys of what I'll call The Great Unspoken Act, I couldn't...make it happen.

You know what I mean. I could rise to the occasion, but I couldn't get the mental porn factory cranking. Couldn't *finish*.

Why? Because I was thinking about Garret. That's my confession. I was throwing a bone for Garret Johnson (who was, at that very moment, in the attic above me, nothing but a foot of beams and plaster between us), and it was freaking me out.

Well, more than that. It was pissing me off.

For one thing, it meant that Judy had been right when she'd made fun of me for circling his face in my yearbook. For another, I sort of felt out of control of the situation, because I didn't *want* to be thinking about him at that particular moment.

Did I?

I wanted to be thinking about Brian Sutton. Or Jacob Lindsey. Or that guy in my art class, Ronnie Palmer, who told really funny jokes and had a knockout smile. Or one of a hundred guys I saw on TV or in the movies. Anyone but Garret Johnson. Why? Because most of my brain had labeled him a weirdo loony oddball freak, and who wanted to fantasize about *that*?

I don't mean to say that I lumped him in with the bullies or jerks. I don't know what I mean to say, actually, except that I was confused, and irritated.

And he hadn't even been in our house for twenty-four hours.

I remembered then that I'd forgotten to look up the word *leer*. What was it he'd said? *Sorry, I can't help but leer. Leer* probably meant the same thing as *sneer*. They rhymed, anyway. I gave up on The Great Unspoken Act and took the dictionary down from the shelf over my desk.

---

[1] **leer** *verb*: to cast a sidelong glance; *esp* to give a leer.

Don't you love it when they use the word you're looking up to define itself? It's like looking up *cow* and having the definition be *a cowlike animal*. I read the second entry.

² **leer** *noun*: a lascivious, knowing, or wanton look.

Knowing, I got, but *lascivious* I was cloudy on. And *wantons* were what they made soup with, right? Wrong.

¹ **wanton** *noun*: one given to self-indulgent flirtation.

Interesting. *Self-indulgent flirtation* sounded a little like The Great Unspoken Act. I flipped back to the Ls.

³ **lascivious** *adjective*: lewd, lustful.

Full stop. Lewd? *Lustful?* He'd apologized for not being able to help looking at me *lustfully*? I'd never been looked at lustfully in my life—not that I knew of, anyway. Maybe it was a word Garret needed to look up, too.

I emerged from my bedroom and stepped out into the hall, glancing at the stairs leading up to the closed attic door. There was no music coming from behind it, no sound of footsteps. *Maybe he's hanging from the ceiling*, I thought. I wandered downstairs, just to see if he'd gotten bold enough to start hanging out with the Renneker clan. Dawn and Trisha were watching a movie and Dad was asleep on the sofa, *Case Studies in Clinical*

Depression laid open across his chest. Judy, I saw through the front window, was in the driveway washing Dexter's car—and doing a half-assed job of it, from what I could tell. She made a couple of swipes across the hood with a sponge and then just stood there waving the hose back and forth, like she was watering the lawn. I went into the kitchen, where Mom sat at the island on a stool, leafing through a catalog.

"Dex," she said without looking up, "I really think we should revisit this decision of yours not to go to college next year."

"Not Dex," I said. "Kyle."

"Oh." She glanced at me over the top of her reading glasses. "Hi, dear. What are you up to?"

Trying to get our houseguest out of my sex fantasies, I thought, but said, "Just hanging out."

"And how *are* you? I mean, what's new?"

This is how it was in our house. There were so many of us, sometimes finding your mom in the kitchen, alone, was like running into an old friend you hadn't spoken to in weeks.

"I'm fine," I said. "Same old."

"School's going okay?"

"Yep."

"And . . ." She seemed to be searching her brain to remember which drama was attached to me. ". . . Any news on the dating front?"

There *was* no "dating front." Had I *ever* had a date with a guy? No, other than my one-time fling with Brent Hartley, which—at his request—I hadn't exactly broadcast. "Not really," I said.

"They don't have one of those gay student support groups at your school, do they?"

I shook my head.

"Well, that's a shame. It would be a great way for you to meet people. Maybe you could start one."

"Mom! I'm not exactly walking around school waving a rainbow flag. You're the one who told me not *everyone* has to know."

"I know I did. It just seems a shame, because there must be other gay students, and it might be nice for you to be acquainted with them."

I could think of quite a few guys at Milton I would like to "be acquainted with"—horizontally. But I knew what she meant. And she was right. A decade from now, I was going to be standing at my ten-year reunion finding out that about a dozen of those hotties were gay, had been gay the whole time, but were too afraid to announce it.

"*Do* you have other gay friends?"

I shrugged. "Just Ian. There are a few guys who I *think* are gay, but no one else I know of, for sure."

"Ian Heller? I didn't know he was gay."

"He came out to his parents before I came out to you. It was like the birth of Queer Duck," I said, thinking of that hilarious cartoon I'd seen where Queer Duck bursts out of his egg, looks at his parents, and sings, "I'm gaaaaaayyyyyy!"

Mom hadn't seen the cartoon. "I don't like that word, 'queer.'"

"Gay people use it all the time."

"Well, that'll take me some getting used to." She looked down at her catalog again and flipped a page. "I don't know why I'm so preoccupied with replacing the countertops. There's nothing wrong with them the way they are now. Hey," she said brightly, looking up again. "Why don't you and Ian date? Have you ever considered it? You're already friends, and you obviously get along."

"Let's not go there," I groaned.

"It's just a thought."

"So," I said, opening the refrigerator, "can I ask you something?"

"Of course."

"Did you ever notice how Judy's meaner to me than she is to anyone else?"

"She shouldn't be being mean, period. Maybe it's just hormones. Teenagers go through a lot of emotional ups and downs when they hit puberty."

I didn't want to think about Judy's hormones. Ick. "She's just been kind of a monster to me for about five years—ever since we all moved back in together."

"Don't call your sister a monster, Kyle. And keep in mind, that year apart was a difficult time for everyone. I'm just glad it's behind us."

I was sorry I'd brought it up. Trying to sound casual, as if the subject held no interest for me, I asked, "So what's your take on Garret?"

"Why? Is he being mean, too?"

"No! I just wondered what you thought of him."

"He's nice. A little strange, but nice."

"So you picked up on the strange thing?"

"Frankly, he's got a bit of Eddie Haskell in him."

"Who's that?"

"Eddie Haskell was a character from an old TV show we used to watch when I was little. He was this boy who used to turn on the charm around grown-ups, and be completely different when they weren't around. I have a feeling the Garret I'm seeing isn't the real one."

Not unless you've seen the one who sleeps in a coffin, I thought. It was tempting to tell her what I'd heard, but I didn't. I wanted to find out more for myself, first.

"But he does seem very sweet," she added.

"Sweet? I don't know if I'd call him that."

"Well, you've barely spoken to him. You haven't even gotten to know him."

"He's hiding out up there. Doesn't want to be 'disturbed,' apparently."

"He's probably just shy," she said. "Tell you what, let's kill two birds with one stone. Will you take Garret's laundry basket up to him, and explain how the laundry system works? I've got him down for Thursday on the schedule. And tell him he's on table-setting duty tonight."

"You're giving him *chores*?"

"I want him to feel like he's part of the family."

"What's the other 'bird' I'm supposed to kill?"

"Well, maybe going up there will give you two a chance to talk, get to know each other a little."

And maybe he'll drain every last drop of blood from my body, turn into a bat, and fly off into the afternoon, I thought, though secretly I was happy to have an excuse to go knock on his door.

"Sure."

"But before you do that, would you please go tell Judy that Sasha called? I didn't know she was right out there in the driveway and told Sasha she wasn't home."

I nodded, and headed out the door that led to the garage.

"Thanks, honey. It was nice talking to you!" she hollered after me, as if there were no telling when our paths might cross again.

I walked through the garage and out into the driveway. Judy's back was to me. She was still facing Dexter's Mustang, still waving the hose back and forth. Having logged an entire summer at Suds, I felt like telling her she wasn't accomplishing anything other than wasting a ton of water. You can't *rinse* a car clean. But I wasn't in the mood to pick a fight.

I walked around one side of her. She looked deep in thought, hypnotized.

"Hey—" I said.

She spun around with the hose, splattering it right across my stomach.

"Jesus!"

As if I'd said the first word of an unfinished sentence, she finished it. "…loves me and is very concerned about you."

"You did that on purpose!"

"I didn't," she said. "It was an accident. *This* is on purpose." She raised the hose and sprayed me again, this time across my chest.

"Cut it out!"

"What do you want?"

"I came out here to give you a phone message, not get soaked!" I said.

"What's the message?"

"Sasha called."

"*Her*. She's probably dying to shriek into my ear about something." She turned back to the car.

"You're welcome," I said, and then changed my mind about not wanting to pick a fight, since she'd sprayed me. "By the way, dirt doesn't just slide off a car when you take a hose to it. You have to do a little work, you know? Use a little elbow grease?"

"Huh," she said matter-of-factly.

I turned and started back into the garage. The hose blasted the middle of my back.

Upstairs, I stopped off in my room, yanked the wet shirt over my head, and dug a dry one out of my dresser. I pulled it on and checked my hair in the mirror. I tried to put a totally bemused, *whatever* expression on my face. Then I carried Garret's laundry basket up to the attic, took a deep breath, and knocked on his door.

"Who is it?"

"Kyle."

A few moments passed. Then I heard his voice again: "Come in."

The door was unlocked. I eased it open. The attic, I thought at first, was on fire. But it wasn't warm, it was just...red. The shades were drawn in the dormer windows, even though it was the middle of the afternoon, and the lightbulbs gave the walls, the ceiling, even the wooden floor a reddish hue. Garret was stretched out on his back on the air hockey table, wearing only a pair of dark jeans. His hands were folded over his chest, and his eyes were closed.

I just stood there holding his laundry basket, waiting for him to move.

"What can I do for you?" he asked without opening his eyes.

"Are you...sleeping...on the air hockey table?"

"More like meditating," he said. "Contemplating." He opened his eyes and rose to a sitting position, then lowered his hands and crossed his legs, Buddha-style. Suddenly, he didn't look like a dead body anymore. He looked like a very much alive—and shirtless—guy. "Is that for me?"

I, who didn't look at any naked or partially clothed guy in the locker room above the kneecaps, was staring at his chest, his bare shoulders, his arms, his nipples, the trail leading...down.

I was getting a real eyeful. Had he been lying around like this on the air hockey table all afternoon, or had he just taken his shirt off and jumped up there when he heard who was at the door? He wasn't at all muscular. He was skinnier than me, even.

God, *I* was the one leering now.

"Is that for me?" he asked again.

I started, and glanced down at the basket. "Yeah. My mom said to bring it up to you and tell you about our laundry system."

"The laundry has a system?"

"Everything has a system around here. You're down for Thursdays, so it just means that on Thursday afternoon, when you get home from school, you bring your dirty clothes and sheets and stuff down to the laundry room and put them in the washer—but don't turn it on, just leave them there. Mom doesn't like anyone but her touching the settings. Then she'll wash them, move them to the dryer, and holler for you when they're done so you can do the folding, if she hasn't already done it herself."

"Efficient," he said. He was staring at me with his head tilted slightly forward. He wasn't leering. But the look he was giving me was intense.

"Yeah, it's a real miracle of science. Oh—also, hate to tell you, but she's decided to give you chores so you'll feel like one of the gang."

"How thoughtful."

"I don't think she's gonna waylay you too hard, though. Tonight you're on table-setting duty." I bounced the basket off my shins. "Your name only has one *T* in it, right?"

"Correct," he said.

I pointed to the handle where Mom had written on it with her new Sharpie. "She spelled it wrong."

"I'll live," Garret said.

A long silence stretched out between us. I was bobbing on my heels, feeling awkward as hell. I set the basket on the floor near the door, and remembered the second bird I was supposed to kill: get to know him. He was so poised, so calm and cool. So...half naked. How, I wondered, did anyone ever "get to know" Garret Johnson?

"You going on Junior Jaunt?" I asked.

"I'm sorry?"

"The trip the juniors are taking. To Colonial Williamsburg. You have to sign up for it by the end of this week if you want to go."

"Oh, I think my mom already signed me up."

It was weird, hearing him mention his mom. I'd met both his parents briefly the day before, but still he didn't seem to be *of* parents. He didn't seem to belong to anyone.

"You?" he asked.

"Yep. I'm going."

"Well," he said with a slight smile, "I'll resume my meditating now. But tonight, after dinner, perhaps you'd like to be my guest so that I might draw your portrait?"

His guest? In my attic, in *my* house? I actually felt frightened by the idea, for some reason—uneasy at the thought of spending a chunk of time with him alone. "I don't know."

"Oh, come on," he said. Then, graceful as a cat, he sprung from the table, walked over to his bed, and picked up his sketch pad. He was flipping through it as he crossed the floor to where I stood. "I drew your sister last night."

He showed me the "portrait." It was sort of like a Jackson Pollock, but in black charcoal: a storm of lines that wandered all over the paper and overlapped and intersected here and there. With a smudging pencil, or his finger, he'd smeared certain areas, and the crazy thing was that out of all that chaos, I thought I *did* see Judy's face. A pretty good likeness, too.

"Judy was up here?"

"Yes."

"She posed for you?"

"It's called 'sitting.' She sat for me."

I felt my face flush with anger and jealousy. I looked up from the portrait and peered around the red-tinged room as if it were a crime scene. My eyes fell on the screen of the Ms. Pac-Man game, where the initials of the highest scorers were blinking: *GHJ, GHJ, JLR, JLR, JLR, GHJ.*

Judy's middle name was Lynn. "What's your middle name?" I asked Garret, turning away from the game.

"Hayden," he said. "What's yours?"

"Brendan." I looked him right in the eye. "Yeah, I'll come up tonight. I'll sit for you. What time?"

"The later the better," he said. "Eleven? I do my best work at night."

Back in my room, I saw the damp shirt draped over the desk chair and got mad at Judy all over again. Not just for spraying me with the hose, but for existing. More specifically, for going up to the attic and "sitting" for Garret and playing Ms. Pac-Man without my knowing about it. Okay, she had the right to go up there if he invited her. It was her house, too. But the thought of it irked me to no end.

I was crossing the room to get my guitar when I caught sight of myself again in the mirror. I saw the image on my T-shirt, reflected backward: Dylan sitting on the curb, holding his Wayfarers, staring into the camera. And that's when I realized why the look Garret had been giving me in the attic had seemed so familiar. It was the same look.

I know what you're about.

I was doomed, I thought, to lust after Garret Johnson.

He aligned the forks and knives on each plate, folded the napkins into swans—a trick he said he'd learned from a cousin who was a caterer—and set them on top of the silverware. (Trisha said it looked like her fork was stabbing her swan, but Mom said the table looked "restaurant fancy.") He *sirred* Dad and *ma'amed* Mom again, until they reminded him he didn't need to do that. He complimented Mom on the spaghetti. He was a model of *un*creepy but over-the-top politeness.

Sunday evening was that weird time that was both part of the weekend and a school night. I was supposed to be in bed by 11 P.M., and so was Judy. At least that meant her bedroom door would be closed when I snuck past it. In fact, all the upstairs doors were closed and everyone was either asleep or pretending to be. I half-expected at least one of those doors to open suddenly, and since I was already a little nervous, if one of them *had* opened, I probably would have jumped about a foot off the floor. But I made it to the attic steps undetected.

Undetected. As if this were an illegal activity. I had to remind myself that I wasn't doing anything wrong, other than not being in bed.

I climbed the steps and tapped lightly on the door.

"Enter," he said, "and abandon all hope."

Again, it was unlocked. I opened it and stepped into the red light. He was shirted this time (a black T-shirt that had the words LIVE LARGE, DIE LARGE ironed onto the front of it), and he was flipping through a schoolbook at the makeshift desk Dad had made for him out of a piece of Masonite and two filing cabinets.

"Why'd you say 'abandon all hope'?" I asked, closing the door behind me.

"Just an expression. Actually, that was an attempt at a joke. I've been told I have a very dry sense of humor."

"I've been told I exaggerate too much."

"Do you?"

I shrugged. "Only about a million times a day."

"Funny," he said, but he wasn't laughing. He closed the book, turned off the desk lamp (the only lightbulb in the attic that wasn't red), and said, "Do you want to do anything, by the way?"

The question froze me in my tracks. Was he talking about fooling around? Then I saw him indicating the games in the attic. By *do*, he meant *play*. "Air hockey," I said, guessing that it was something Judy hadn't played. The attic felt tainted by her previous day's presence. I didn't need to put myself in the position of worrying about whether or not I could squeeze her initials out of one of those "high score" slots on the video games. "I think it'll be too loud, though," I told him. "People are asleep downstairs."

"Are you breaking curfew?"

"I don't have a curfew. I'm just, you know, supposed to be in bed by eleven on a school night."

"Then I'm honored to have you risking your neck by coming up here."

Interesting word choice, I thought. "Where should I sit?"

"Wherever you like. Why don't you sit on my bed? That's probably the most comfortable spot."

I passed the video games and the giant television screen (I was tempted to ask him to turn it on just to see how it looked, but I didn't) and sat down on his bed. It was meticulously made, as if he hadn't slept on it the night before. He carried the desk chair over and set it down a few feet away, then got his sketch pad and box of charcoals from beside the desk.

"Is this where Judy sat?" I asked, looking down at the bed.

"Same spot exactly. Hold still, will you?" He crossed his legs, balanced the sketch pad on his knee, took out a piece of charcoal, and gave me a long, serious stare. Then he started drawing.

The attic was so quiet, you could hear the sound of the charcoal scraping over the paper. He looked up at me and down at the pad, up at me and down. "So," he said, "ask me what you want to ask me."

"What do you mean?"

"Since I arrived, any time we've been in the same room together, you've been staring at me pretty hard." What was closer to the truth was that *he'd* been looking at *me* pretty heavily. Then again, for me to know that, I guess I had to have been looking at him, too. He said, "There's a reason for that, and I can probably guess what it is."

This was going in one of two directions. I decided to choose which one. "Coover warned me against you."

His drawing hand stopped moving. He stared down at the sketch pad for a moment. Then he started drawing again. "Ah, yes," he said. "Coover."

"He told me what you told him. Or—what he *says* you told him."

"You know, I've been in and out of a lot of schools over the years, and every one of them has a Coover."

"Why have you been to so many schools?" I asked.

"Because of my dad's job. He opens prefab housing plants for this company called Presley-Landis. Meaning, he goes to where the new branch is about to open, hires the staff, gets the business up and running for its first year or so. Then he goes off and does it all over again someplace else—and takes us with him. I've lived in four different states in the past five years. I've gone to six different schools."

"Do you like moving around so much?"

"Besides," he said, ignoring the question, "for the record, I didn't reveal anything to Coover. He intuited it, and asked me directly. All I did was confirm what he'd intuited."

"What was that?" I asked.

A cell phone rang somewhere very close to me. I looked around, but didn't see one anywhere. "Sorry," he said. He set the sketch pad down, came over to where I was sitting, and dug the phone out from beneath his pillow. "Hello?"

I watched him turn away and begin pacing the floor.

"I understand," he said into the phone. "I do. One of the mortals is here right now, in fact. I'm sure he can spare a few pints, but I'm not hungry at the moment.... *Yes*, I'm getting enough to eat. We had some very nice spaghetti tonight.... I'm fully aware that tomato sauce and blood aren't the same thing, thank you very much, Helena.... Have I transformed? Not since I got here.... Because I haven't been in the mood to fly, that's why. Listen, I've got to go. We can talk about this later."

He hung up and glanced at me.

I felt a tightness in my forehead and realized my brow was raised. My mouth was ajar, too. I must have looked dumbfounded.

"I can explain that," he said.

"You...don't have to," I said.

"Well, I might as well, since we were already on the subject." He walked back over to the chair and sat down, but he didn't pick up the sketch pad. With utter seriousness, he peered at me and said, "What Coover intuited is that I am...vampiric."

Was *vampiric* even a word? He seemed to be waiting for me to respond. "You're a vampire," I said. I sounded ridiculous, saying it out loud in a serious voice.

"In training," he clarified.

"Bullshit."

"Such language," he said. "But listen, I don't want you to be uncomfortable. I'm not going to harm anyone here."

For all the sarcastic, vampire-related remarks I'd made to myself over the past few days, I realized now that I'd never really thought it was true. I *still* didn't think it was true. In a twisted way, I thought he was trying to make fun of me. "What do you get out of this act?" I asked him.

"I don't expect you to believe me. And I don't expect to have to prove anything to you. It is what it is."

It is what it is. Talk about looking up a word and finding it used as its own definition.

"That person on the phone?" he said. "That was Helena. My

Lestat, if you will. You've read—or seen—*Interview with the Vampire*?"

I nodded. I'd seen the movie.

"Helena's the person who made me what I am, and who's training me to become what I'm...meant to be."

"So you're really a vampire," I said, trying to sound like I believed anything but.

"Yes." He raised an open palm. "I hope that doesn't disturb you."

"No," I said, "it's great. We had a zombie living up here just last month. And a wolfman before that." Suddenly, I felt guilty—as if he'd just admitted he was terminally ill and I was making fun of cancer patients. But then I thought: *Why should I feel guilty? It's an act.* What I felt more than anything was annoyed. My question was still very much alive in my head: *What do you get out of all this?* "Well, if you *are*...what you say you are...why would you tell a guy like Coover? He's a serious nutcase."

"I know. Coover does seem more dangerous than most. But I just couldn't be dishonest. It would have been demeaning. I'm sure you know what that's like."

"What do you mean?"

"Judy told me you're out about being gay. You wouldn't relish having to *deny* it, would you? Wouldn't that make you feel... ashamed?"

"Yeah, but I really *am* gay. You can't tell me, *seriously*, that you believe what you say. About yourself, I mean." I was everything at once: guilty, annoyed, uncomfortable, and—okay, I'll admit it—intrigued. Why else would I have agreed to come up here?

Garret folded his arms over his lap, huffed lightly, and smiled at me. Duh. That was also the reason I'd agreed to come up here. He looked kissable beyond belief.

Still, my feeling annoyed and uncomfortable won out. "Are you done with your portrait?"

"Almost," he said, reaching for the sketch pad and charcoal. He started making a few more lines. "Judy told me something else about you."

"What's that?"

"Well, let's just say—hold still, now—let's just say she revealed that you have some grudge against me…*and* an interest in me that seems to go beyond your curiosity about what I am."

"I don't know what you're talking about."

"She said you resent my being up here, occupying your game room. And that you have the hots for me."

Thank you, Monster. Thank you a lot. Feeling the anger boiling up in me, I said, "Let me tell you about Judy. She's *mean*, okay? She's got it in for me, for some reason. Ever since she found Jesus, or whatever—way before that, even—she's been mean. She'd say *anything* if she thought it would make me look stupid."

"So you'd look stupid if you had the hots for me?"

"That's not what I meant."

"Well, which is it? Do you have the hots for me, or not?"

I didn't like being put on the spot. "Are you *done*?" I asked.

He lifted the charcoal and looked down at the sketch pad. "Actually, I am. I don't think I'll smudge this one. It looks fine the way it is." He turned the pad around to show me the portrait.

It was a crazy mess of lines. One giant scribble filling up the page. But there, emerging from that chaos of charcoal strokes, was *me*.

"I have to get to sleep," I told him, pushing up from the bed.

"Later, then—another night," he said, almost making it sound like a question.

"Another night for what?"

"The chance to draw you again."

"Maybe," I said, and headed for the door.

In my room, unsure of whether or not he was overhead talking on his cell phone to Helena—his "Lestat"—or lying flat on the air hockey table, or giving any thought at all to *me*, I went to bed that night trying to think about anything other than Garret Johnson.

But I dreamed about him.

I dreamed I was in my bed, just on the verge of falling asleep, when I heard a faint tapping at one of my windows.

I sat up. The curtains were drawn, but I could make out a dark shape on the other side. This was pretty frightening because my room was on the second floor, the roof sloped sharply, and it was impossible for someone—or something—to *stand* outside my window.

Cautiously, I got out of bed and walked over to the curtains. The shape was moving. Hovering. I drew the curtains back and felt my heart jerk up toward the bottom of my throat.

Garret was floating there, looking directly at me through the glass. His hair was slicked back, his skin looked bluish in the moonlight, and his eyes seemed to glow. He was still dressed in jeans and his Live Large, Die Large T-shirt, and I expected to see batlike wings sprouting from his shoulders. But there weren't any wings. He just drifted there, upright, about a foot away from the house, looking at me with that cool *I-know-what-you're-about* expression on his face.

I opened the window. "What the hell are you doing?" I asked.

"I just wanted to tell you, I hope you weren't too uncomfortable earlier."

"How come you can float? Is this you…transforming?"

"No. This is nothing. A parlor trick. Transforming is a whole other thing entirely. But listen, don't worry about anything."

"I'm not worried," I said. "But this is pretty weird. I mean, you could have just come downstairs and knocked."

"Maybe I'm trying to impress you."

"I'm impressed," I said.

"You're a cool guy, Kyle."

"Thanks."

"I've grown very fond of you quite quickly."

"I…I like you, too."

"I want you," he said, and smiled, revealing a pair of incisors nearly an inch long.

I was terrified. And excited. "Okay," I said.

"But not just yet," he added.

"W-why?"

"Because you have to be sure you want *me*."

I was sure. This was a dream and nothing really counted, and so I was absolutely, positively sure.

But he closed his mouth, then gave me a wry smile and drifted back up to the attic. Leaning out, I saw him fly straight in through one of the open dormer windows.

When my alarm went off, I was humping the mattress.

6. JUDY:
Testify, sister, testify!

So Job died,'" Tina read aloud, "'being old and full of days.'" She closed her bible—hers was oversize and bound in white leather, with a picture of Jesus embossed on the front—and said, "Amen," as if she'd just finished a prayer.

"Amen," the rest of them said.

Jacob smiled at her proudly. She smiled back. I tried to burn a hole through her forehead with my glare. "What did you think about the reading, Noelle?" Jacob asked.

"I liked it because it had a happy ending," she said in her mousy little voice. "He got to live to be an old man."

"Yeah," Dwayne said. "And he got all his stuff back, plus some. That was pretty cool."

Jacob nodded, still smiling, and turned to me. "Judy?"

Hello? I wanted to say to him. *Have you noticed the strawberry shade I spent two hours putting into my hair? Have you noticed my* *new blouse? My new shoes?* He wasn't even looking at me, having asked me what I thought. "'Plus some'?" I repeated. "God gave Job a *thousand* donkeys and *six thousand* camels! *Fourteen thousand* sheep!* He went overboard in the 'plus some' department, if you ask me. I mean, how's Job supposed to *feed* all those animals?"

"They can graze," Dwayne said.

"Yeah, but they'll need water, too. And medical attention. And can you even imagine what fourteen thousand sheep *smell* like?"

I was doing it again. Breaking through the rubberhead, being myself. The four of them were staring at me as if I were committing sacrilege. "Of course," I added, "Noelle's right, it *was* a happy ending, and it's a real lesson for all of us about being patient when God starts destroying our lives for no reason."

Jacob cleared his throat. He turned back to Tina. "You read that last chapter with real feeling."

"Thank you," she breathed.

I stared down at my open bible and read silently, *"Canst thou draw out leviathan with an hook? Or his tongue with a cord which thou lettest down? Canst thou put an hook into his nose? Or bore his jaw through with a thorn?"*

Thou canst do all of those things, I thought. *To Tina.*

It had been a week since the Saturday night when I'd seen her car parked in front of Jacob's house, a week since I'd gotten so angry at both of them that I'd marched up to the attic and let Garret draw my portrait. I'd promised myself that I wouldn't mention having seen Tina's car to Jacob, in part because it would mean having to admit that I'd driven past his house for no good reason, and in part because I'd promised myself that I'd play fair, keep things on the up-and-up as much as possible. But listening to the two of them talk about Job and God and Satan, and watching their mutual fanfest, I couldn't take it any longer. When Tina walked off to use the bathroom and Jacob's dad appeared, beer in hand, and led Dwayne and Noelle out to the garage to show them his doorknob collection, I got up and took the chair Tina had been using, right next to where Jacob was sitting, leafing through his bible.

Leaning into him, I whispered, "I think Tina's faking it."

He pulled his head back, confused. "Faking what?"

"The whole religious thing. I don't think she really believes in what the bible says—in the story of Job, or any of it. I don't even think she believes in God."

"Judy, what are you talking about?"

I shushed him. "I'm just telling you for your own good. My theory is that she's only attending your study group because she has a crush on you. It's so dishonest. I just don't want to see you get hurt."

"Nobody's going to hurt me," he whispered back. "I don't know why you'd say that about Tina. She and I have had long talks about the bible, and about Jesus—"

"I know she was here last Saturday night." It slipped right

out, like water from a glass. So much for my promise to myself. I could see the hesitation in his face and I barreled forward, trying to make the most of it. "I had to...deliver a prescription to my aunt—who lives nearby?—and I just happened to be coming down your road and saw Tina's car parked out front. On *Saturday night*. Your homework night. Your I-have-to-be-by-myself-to-work-on-my-paper night. You two had a secret bible study, didn't you? Or a date?"

The hesitation in his face didn't hold for long. It was already dissolving into irritation. "We didn't have a bible study," he said. "It turns out, she knows a lot about the Medicis because she did a presentation on them last year in her humanities class, so she came over and we...talked."

"About the meta-cheese?"

"Yeah."

"I still think she's hiding something."

"*Who's* hiding something?" That breathy voice drifted down from above us. Tina was back from the bathroom, standing less than a foot away. "I hope you weren't talking about me," she said, looking oddly delighted.

"It was a private conversation."

"It sounded intense, whatever the topic was."

"The topic was stupid," I said. *"Boring."* I reached a hand into the bowl of potato chips on the coffee table.

"Ooh," she said, "you might want to go easy on those."

"And you might want your butt kicked up between your shoulder blades," I snapped.

"Whoa!" Jacob stood. "Let's just..." He closed the bible, set it down on his chair, and said, "Judy, can we—can I talk to you outside for a minute?"

Tina was smiling and Jacob was all stern-faced, and I could feel my own face flush with rage and embarrassment. I turned and walked straight out of the house. He followed me. When we were on the front porch, I stopped and folded my arms, but he kept going, so I did, too, until the two of us were standing in the middle of the front yard.

He opened and closed his mouth a few times without saying anything, and when he finally spoke, he worked his hands around an invisible football he was about to toss out of the ballpark. "You and I aren't...dating. We agree on that, right?"

"What's that supposed to mean?"

"Just that we agree: We never decided to date. And, in fact, we've never even *gone* on a date."

"So?"

"I just want to make sure we're both clear on that."

"I have eyes. I have ears. I know we're not dating."

"Okay," he said. "Good."

"You're not dating Tina, are you?"

"That's something else I want to talk to you about."

"You *are* dating her! I knew it! I could see her sinking her claws into you—"

"I'm not saying we *are* or *aren't* dating. I'm saying it's not really your business to get bent out of shape about it." He

sounded stern, but a little nervous, too. "Listen, the point is, you've got to get over this bad feeling you have for Tina. It's not good for the group."

"Do I have to *like* everyone in the group?"

"Well, no. But it helps. It's not good to have all that negativity floating around when we're trying to learn more about the teachings of Christ."

God, he was cute when he talked about religion. He had this little boy face that looked like the most sincere thing that could ever exist. Then I thought of Tina kissing that face and wanted to scream.

"I think I can learn about Jesus *and* not like Tina. I think I'm emotionally capable of that."

"Fine, but you've got to keep the negativity to yourself. I mean, what *was* that in there about how you think she's faking? Tina's not faking anything. And — I'm sorry, I don't mean this as a criticism — but you're the one who doesn't go to church. If anyone in our study group might seem to be 'faking,' as you put it, it would be you."

Boy, *that* one backfired on me big-time.

"Not that I'm saying you are," he added. "I'm just saying, people who live in glass houses shouldn't...you know..."

"Throw stones," I said. The expression had never made sense to me. Was it about vulnerability or hypocrisy? Don't throw the stones while you're standing inside your house because obviously you'll break your walls, or don't throw stones because people might throw them back?

I was still standing with my arms folded over my stomach. The rubberhead was completely gone. What Kyle would have called the Monsterface had taken over. I stared at Jacob for a moment while he looked back, calmly waiting to see if what he'd said had sunk in.

"What church did you say you go to again?" I asked.

One afternoon a few days later, Dexter came home from school and said he was going to make a mall run, and I asked him if I could come along. I'd tried on all of my dresses and couldn't stand the way I looked in them—one made me look slutty, one made me look frumpy, one made me look fat; none of them was the look I was aiming for: sexy, yet respectable; hot, yet... holier-than-Tina.

"Sure," Dexter said, "come along. But I'm leaving, like, five minutes ago."

We were standing in the kitchen. Garret was within earshot, in the laundry room folding his clothes. To my amazement, he leaned out into the open doorway and asked if he could join us. I'd already gotten pretty used to his staying hidden away in the attic.

"The more the mallier," Dexter said, reaching for his keys.

The mall had been built a few years ago, smack in the middle of what used to be farmland. It looked superimposed in the middle of a giant field, surrounded by a moat of parking lot. As we walked in through the food court, Dexter said he wanted to go to Radio Shack and Athletic Mongoose (where Mac Prentice had offered him the job that was tempting him away from college). He also had a thing for Beth Garland, a girl who worked at Athletic Mongoose—which, now that I thought about it, may have been part of his motivation for wanting to take the job. Those stores were all on the first level, and the dress shops I wanted to look at were on the second. "Want to meet back here in an hour?" I asked him.

"Sounds good," he said. "Later." He rounded the corner of the Goody-Goody yogurt shop and was gone.

I turned and looked at Garret. "What about you? Got some shopping to do?"

"Actually, no."

"Why'd you want to come, then?"

He shrugged and tucked his narrow hands into the pockets of his tight, ratty jeans. "It's fun to observe the mortals now and again."

"You didn't bring your sketch pad," I observed.

"I can sketch in my mind, if I feel like it."

I glanced around the food court, lined with potted trees, some of which had tiny birds flitting around the branches (did the poor things live their entire lives in a *mall*?) and then looked back at Garret, who seemed content just to stare at me.

"So…do you want to come with me?" I asked.

"I'd be delighted."

"*Delighted?* I'm shopping for dresses, you know."

"I'll be glad to assist in any way I can."

"Do you talk like that on purpose?" I asked as we were walking toward the escalator.

"Like what?"

"Like some lord of the manor."

"I wasn't aware I sounded like a lord of anything, but I'll take it as a compliment."

We stood side by side as the escalator carried us up the middle of one wing of the mall. Down below, an old man sat on a bench, dropping and catching a red rubber ball over and over again.

I took us into one of the small boutique shops first. The prices were way out of my range, but I wanted to see what was out there. That was a mistake, of course, because every dress I saw, I wanted. (I really only had about forty dollars to spend—all that was left of my birthday money after my latest makeover spree.)

"This one's lovely," Garret said, holding up a sleek black dress with gold thread woven through it.

"Uh-huh. Three hundred bucks' worth of lovely. I think I need to get realistic." I led us to another, larger store that was a little more reasonably priced. We strolled around the racks, looking at the merchandise.

Garret held up a dress. "How about this one?"

"That's an *evening* gown," I said, eyeing the red silk.

"Well, what's the occasion? Junior Jaunt?"

"Huh?" I'd practically forgotten about that stupid field trip coming up the next Friday. "No, I'm not going formal for Colonial Williamsburg. This is for church. And I've only got forty dollars to work with."

"Oh, well, why didn't you say so? We're in the wrong store." He put his hand on my shoulder, steered me back out into the mall, and led the way to T.J.Maxx.

"You're probably right," I said, once we were there and looking at a few price tags.

"So, you're taking this religion thing a step further."

"Of course. My religious belief is very important to me."

"What church are you attending?"

"First Baptist."

"Ever been before?"

I shook my head.

"Your dress won't matter. They're going to put you in a white robe and dunk you in a pool."

"*What?*"

"Newcomers get baptized," he said calmly. "Everyone knows that."

He was kidding, I thought. I wasn't falling for it. "Nobody's dunking me in anything."

"Don't say I didn't warn you."

"How would you know, anyway? I didn't think your kind spent a lot of time in churches."

"Touché. We don't." He let out a little laugh. "They'd probably dunk me and hold my head under till I drowned."

"But that wouldn't kill you, would it? Aren't you supposed to be immortal? Or maybe the preacher's hand would burn your flesh."

"Such presumption."

"Just asking," I said. I was still waiting for him to break this facade, to come clean. He studied the dresses with great seriousness, and pulled a light blue one off the rack. It had a white collar and little white buttons running down the front of it.

"Perfect," he said, examining the price tag. "What's your size?"

I tried it on. He was right; it was perfect. I looked nice—both respectable and sexy at once. Take that, Convertible Girl.

"It flatters you," Garret said, when I stepped out of the dressing room.

"You think so? Thanks."

"I take it you know someone who attends this church."

"Why?"

"Either that, or you're dressing up to impress God. *Do* you know someone there?"

"Maybe," I said, looking at myself in the mirror.

"The leader of your bible study, perhaps? What's his name? Jacob?"

I looked at his reflection. "How do you know about Jacob?"

"Kyle told me."

"It's none of Kyle's business. Or yours. But, yes, Jacob does go to First Baptist. What else did Kyle tell you?"

"Just that he thinks you have a crush on the guy."

Was Kyle onto me? "Kyle's nosy. And gay," I added, for no reason.

"So you've said. Do you believe your brother's going to hell for being gay?"

"I don't care *where* he goes. Why are we even talking about this? And how come I can see your reflection in the mirror, if you're what you say you are? Aren't you supposed to not reflect?"

"That's a movie myth. Obviously I reflect." He waved at me, proving he was there. Deeper in the mirror, I saw a figure glide between two of the racks, then glide back. *Store security?* I wondered. If so, the guy was undercover because he had on a striped T-shirt and jeans.

I paid for the dress, had five dollars and change left to spare, and was in a generous mood. Since Garret had helped me shop, I offered to buy him a slice of pizza in the food court.

We were sitting at a table under one of the potted trees, eating and watching the birds jump around, when the guy in the striped shirt appeared again. He was walking fast, heading straight for us, and this time I recognized him as Ferris Coover.

His hair sported a fresh, dorky-looking flattop. He had his eyes narrowed down to a squint and a crimp in his mouth. As he got closer (I had full view of him while Garret, who was facing the other way, didn't), he reached into one of his pockets and brought out something he immediately started twisting with both hands. He walked right up to Garret and thrust his hands forward.

"Hey!" I said. I didn't know what was going on but knew it couldn't be good.

Garret flinched and stood up. When he turned around to face Coover, I saw that the back of his T-shirt was soaking wet down the middle. "What the hell do you think you're doing?" he asked.

"Destroying you!" Coover seethed. "Ridding Milton of evil!"

"What did you just spill on me? Is it paint?" He tried to look at his own back, then glanced at me. "Did this idiot just ruin my shirt?"

"It looks like water," I said.

"From Lourdes," Coover clarified. He waved the bottle, which was clear plastic and shaped like a little statue of the Virgin Mary. "My aunt filled up twelve of these when she went there. It's burning you alive, isn't it?"

"No," Garret snapped. "You're such a moron. It's not water from Lourdes but *holy water* that's supposed to kill me. And guess what? *That* doesn't kill me, either." He glanced at me. "More movie myth. Child's play." He swung around and took a step toward Coover, who jumped back. "Stay the hell away from me, understand?"

"You're evil," Coover hissed. "You need to die."

"And you need to get a life," Garret told him. "Jesus."

"Don't even say that name," Coover said, backing away. "That name should melt your tongue."

"Well, it doesn't, okay? Jesus, Jesus, Jesus," Garret said, and then leaned forward and stuck his tongue out for Coover to see. I couldn't help it; I started laughing.

"I'll get you," Coover said. "I will." But he was still backing away, and, a moment later, he turned around and practically ran for the glass doors that led out to the parking lot.

Garret snapped his wet shirt away from his back and looked at me, both irritated and astounded. "Welcome to my world."

"Hey, you asked for it," I said, still laughing, thinking maybe this was the moment he was finally going to come clean about his vampire act.

But he said, "I didn't *ask* for it. Well, maybe I did. I never should have told him anything about myself."

You never should have lied, maybe? I thought of saying.

But he only snapped at his shirt again, glared toward the parking lot, and said, "It's a form of persecution, you know, and it's wrong."

First Baptist is in Lewiston—a ten-minute drive from Milton. The following Sunday, I took a shower, did my hair (and redid it about four times until it didn't look like an old broom), put on makeup, which I almost never wear (and redid *that* a half-dozen times until I stopped looking like an extra from *The Nutcracker*), and buttoned myself up in my new dress. It was only then that I realized I didn't have any blue or white shoes other than sneakers, so I went downstairs to Mom's closet and rifled through about a hundred pairs of her shoes until I found ones that might work. But they were too big, so I ended up stuffing the toes with toilet paper. I could walk, but not with much confidence. So I was batting a thousand by the time I got behind the wheel of Dad's car—which he thankfully let me borrow because he was watching a football game.

The shoe delay had me on the verge of being late. I had to park two blocks away, then hobble up the sidewalk and the steps leading to the front doors, where a pair of suited men who looked like bodyguards smiled but eyed me with suspicion, as if they knew I wasn't supposed to be there. But it's church, right? It's open to the public. What were they going to do, stop me and ask, *Are you Baptist? Can we see your membership card?* I smiled at them and stepped inside.

Imagine a football stadium (well, half a football stadium), except instead of plastic seats and metal railings, everything's made out of plaster and dark wood. And instead of a bunch of loud losers wearing face paint and holding beers, there are all these people dressed in nice clothes, holding bibles or hymnbooks, whispering to one another. Someone's playing an organ, and for all I know, I've stepped into a funeral. But there's no casket. There's a giant, Jesus-less cross behind the pulpit, a choir sitting off to one side, a couple of microphones fixed to podiums, and tall, skinny speakers attached to the walls on either side of the room.

I stood off to one side, watching people slide into and across the pews, filling them up. I peeled my eyes for Jacob's red head of hair. What I saw, instead, was a splash of bright yellow. Tina's dress—the same color as her convertible. She was sitting near the back of the church, in the middle of a half-empty pew. Jacob was beside her, his head bowed down (either praying or reading). I started walking toward them, and Tina noticed me long before I got there. The shock on her face was almost worth the trip. She looked like she was seeing a ghost. She elbowed Jacob, who lifted his head, followed her stare, and spotted me. He didn't look quite as surprised to see me, and he didn't exactly look displeased, either. In fact, he smiled at me. I smiled back, hobbled down the pew, gave Tina the kind of hug you'd give a frail old woman with osteoporosis, and Jacob the kind of hug you'd give Jacob, then sat down next to him, so that he was between us.

"What brings *you* out?" Tina asked. She was smiling now, too, but her eyes were set open a little too wide; she was pissed off and I couldn't have been happier about it.

"The love of the Lord," I told her. Why not go whole-hog? "The love of the Lord compelled me to come."

"How nice for you," she said.

"I'm glad you're here," Jacob told me. "You look great." I noticed that Tina had scooted a little closer to him; her knee, under the folds of her yellow dress, was touching his. I slid over a few inches and pressed my own knee against his other leg.

So there we were: a Jacob Sandwich. And I was feeling pretty cocky. Everybody stood up, the choir started singing, and Jacob was all about me—showing me which hymnal to open, finding the page for me, smiling as he sang. (Maybe his one flaw: The poor cutie is tone-deaf; I'd rather hear Bob Dylan squawking away, and that's saying a *lot*.) I had no idea what the song was, but I sort of lip-synched, and as I did, I glanced over at Tina, who was staring straight ahead and belting out the verses like she was singing a battle cry.

So that's the picture: Tina's mad, Jacob's glad to see me, I'm getting *lots* of attention from him, and I'm on top of the world.

And where can you go, once you've reached the top of the world? What's the only direction left, unless you have your own spaceship?

After some yammering on from the preacher, and some yammering on from the sub-preacher or deacon or whoever, and after some more singing and hand-clapping, things all of the sudden turned serious. "Welcome," the preacher said into one of the microphones for maybe the hundredth time. "I welcome each and every one of you here today. It's so nice to see you." Then he said, "Let me see a show of hands. How many of you are here with us at First Baptist for the very first time?"

I froze. Jacob pointed to me, then took hold of my hand—the first time he'd ever held it—and raised it into the air. There were about a dozen other people in the congregation with their hands raised. I wanted to slip down beneath the pew in front of me and disappear.

"That's fantastic," the preacher said. "Simply fantastic. I wonder if we could do something special today."

I wonder if we can't, I was thinking. *I wonder if we can shut the hell up.* Jacob still had my hand raised in the air.

"I'd like each one of you new folks to come down here and join me. Just come on down and stand here beside me on the stage, and we'll say a special prayer together, a welcoming prayer, one that will weave you into our family, and you can each tell us your name, and what it means to you, personally, to have Christ in your life."

For a moment, no one who had his—or her—hand raised moved.

Then the preacher smiled broadly, swung the fist that wasn't holding the microphone up into the air, and cried out, "Come on, people! Feel the spirit! Get on down here and praise the Lord!" and one by one they stood and moved toward the aisles.

"Go on," Jacob whispered. He looked genuinely happy that this was happening. So did Tina, but for different reasons, I was sure.

"I don't know," I whispered back. "I'm not really good in front of an audience."

"You can do it," he said, squeezing my hand. "It's now or never."

He was right about that.

So, wanting to do anything but, I stood. Jacob let go of my hand, and I started down the pew toward the aisle.

It was as if the dozen of us had been hypnotized. We were all walking slowly, converging on the stage. And I felt as if I was going to topple over at any moment, because I was so nervous and because my feet were swimming around inside my mom's shoes (the toilet paper had been flattened and wasn't doing any good).

Come on, I thought, *you've faked it this far. You can do this. What's the big deal? Just stand up there and talk into a microphone about Jesus in front of two hundred strangers.*

But it just wasn't in me. It wasn't *me.* I wasn't this person, in this ridiculous dress, wearing these ridiculous shoes, wobbling down a church aisle toward a microphone.

Halfway there, I turned around and walked—as quickly as those shoes would allow—back up the aisle. I kept my eyes on the red carpeted floor in front me, kept my gaze away from all the faces, especially Jacob's and Tina's, and didn't stop walking until I was behind the wheel of the car, fumbling to get the key into the ignition.

Dad was on the sofa, still watching the football game, when I got home. It sounded like a party was going on upstairs.

"Back so soon?" he asked, looking at his watch. "I thought the Catholics were the ones who kept it short."

"We ended early. The preacher got Montezuma's revenge."

Somebody scored—not Dad's team, I gathered, because he winced. "What was that you said?"

"Nothing. What's going on up there?" I heard a lot of thumping and hollering coming from upstairs.

"Garret has surrendered the game room for the afternoon. They're all up there, going to town. Even your mother. Tommy's teaching her to play air hockey."

"Garret's up there, too?"

"No. He's in the backyard, trimming the hedges."

"You're making him do lawn work? I thought he was a guest."

"He *is* a guest. But he offered. He insisted, in fact. I said I was going to do it during halftime, but he said he'd be 'delighted' to do it himself so that I could enjoy the show. He's a very *courteous* young man."

"He sure is," I said.

"Your mother thinks it's an act. So do I, but who am I to complain if it gets the hedges trimmed?"

A referee blew a whistle on the screen. A yellow flag flew through the air, and Dad leaned forward and planted his hands on his knees. "Oh, *come on!*"

It was amazing how football could turn even the most bookwormish psychologist into a guy from a beer commercial.

I walked through the kitchen to the back door. When I stepped out onto the patio, I saw that the hedge lining the right side of the yard hadn't been touched yet. Garret was barely a third of the way down the hedge on the left side, delicately snipping away. He was practically doing it one leaf at a time.

He glanced at me as I approached and said, "The prodigal churchgoer returns."

"Why don't you just use nail clippers? It might go faster."

"This is called *finesse*," he said, making a small swipe at a branch. "So how was it? Did they dunk you?"

"Don't ask."

I wasn't about to tell him—or any of them—the whole story. I already felt like the biggest loser imaginable. I couldn't imagine having *any* shot left at Jacob now, couldn't imagine even being able to look at him in school. *Maybe I can lie and say I had a stomachache,* I thought. *Or a panic attack. That's it, I was so close to realizing Jesus's love in my life that I panicked and fled the church....*

Who was I kidding? I'd blown it, big-time. I'd tried for Jacob and lost him. And I hated losing.

I watched Garret clip, clip, clip at the leaves. "Did you really mean it when you said this dress flatters me?" I asked.

"Of course," he said. "And it's obvious. You look stunning."

I smiled at him. I didn't feel like smiling, but I felt like getting somebody to smile at *me*. He did, just barely: that strange, sexy curve of his lips, like he was thinking something mildly devious. I glanced toward the house, then took a step closer to him. "I'll tell you a secret if you tell me one."

He made one more snip at the hedge, then lowered the clippers. "You first."

I reached out and plucked a dark green leaf, and for a few moments I just played with it—ran it over my nose and lips and chin. I bit it in half and then spit it onto the ground. "I'm not really a religious person."

"No?" He didn't seem as surprised as he should have been. But he did seem interested. "So why all the bible-studying and churchgoing? Why the Jesus over your dresser and the cross over your bed?"

When have you ever been in my room? I wondered. Had he been snooping when no one else was around? "What you said the other day? About my having a crush on Jacob, the boy who runs the study? It's true."

"I see. That came from Kyle, remember."

"Well, it *was* true. I had a crush on Jacob, and so I pretended to be saved so I could get to know him and land him as my boyfriend."

"And do you believe in Jesus—at all?"

I shrugged. "How would I know? I've never met the man."

"And God? Do you believe in God?"

I shrugged again. "Maybe there's a God, maybe it's all chaos. Maybe God *is* the chaos. My point is, I made it all up and I've been pretending, just so I could get closer to Jacob. Nobody knows but my friend Sasha. And now you."

"So what's going on with Jacob?"

"That's private."

"Well, that's the *real* story," he said.

"No. The real story is what I just told you. So what's *your* real story?"

"What do you mean?"

"Your. Real. Story," I said. "Let's have it."

"I think I've been fairly up front with you about who and what I am."

"Fairly, maybe. How about completely?"

"Why are you so hostile toward Kyle?" he suddenly asked.

I felt like I was sitting at dinner with my family, with several different conversations darting around the table. "What has that got to do with anything? And who said I was hostile?"

"He did."

"Don't change the subject," I said. "I just told you something very private about myself. Now I'm asking *you* to come clean with *me*. I know you like me." I was reaching. *Leading*. But after the day I'd had, I was desperate. "I can tell by the way you look at me. You told me twice that this dress flatters me."

"*You* brought it up the second time."

He was playing hard to get, but I didn't mind. Just talking to him was making me feel better than I had walking out of that church. "You said you wanted to draw me again."

"I do," Garret said.

"Well? When and where?"

"In the attic, of course."

"The attic is occupied."

"And I have to finish these hedges."

We both looked up toward the roof of the house, where, at that moment, nearly all of my enormous family was lost in game mania.

Garret sighed. "They can't go at it forever, one supposes. How about tonight—say around eleven?"

7. K Y L E :
Mazed and confused

Instead of having to go to any classes on the morning of Junior Jaunt, we all gathered at the side of the building nicknamed Bus Alley. There were four buses for the trip to Williamsburg, and I made sure I was on the one Garret was riding. Judy made sure *she* was on it, too. And because Judy was there, her friend Sasha was there. And because I was there, Ian was there. And by some stroke of fortune that benefited nobody, Ferris Coover was on our bus as well. He sat in the back row where, I presumed, he could keep his creepy eye on us all.

The driver was a dusty-haired old woman named Mrs. Dresden who had baggy arms and bad posture, and who didn't seem to care what we did, so there was a lot of moving around during the hour-and-a-half ride. I spent the first leg of the trip next to Ian on a seat with bad springs that had us tilted away from each other.

"So that's him?" he asked under his breath, looking across

the aisle and up a little ways to where Garret sat next to a girl I didn't know.

"Yep. I'm sure you've seen him around."

"I have. And you lied."

"About what?"

"About whether 'cute' or 'not cute' factored into the equation. He's totally cute. Cute dipped in goth and rolled in . . . hot. What's he look like out of his clothes?"

"I've seen him without his shirt, not naked."

"He's in your gym class, isn't he?"

"Yeah, but I told you, I try not to look at guys in the locker room."

"Oh, yeah. That one'll never make sense to me. You're the most *un*gay gay person I know."

"I'm the *only* gay person you know. And *I'm* the one who's had sex, remember?"

"Rub it in. Rub in the fact that I'll die in Milton a fat, bald virgin."

"Shut up. You said you're moving to New York. And getting a toupee."

"I keep forgetting. Anyway, has he sucked you yet?"

"*What?!*" I burst out laughing and pushed him sideways, making him lean even farther away on the seat.

"Your blood, I mean."

I'd told Ian about the vampire business the day after I'd first heard it myself. It hadn't fazed him one bit. "Mary," he'd said, "we all need to have *something* going on."

"I would have told you if there was *any* kind of sucking taking place, believe me," I said now.

"Well, there's an agenda there, believe me," Ian said, eyeing the back of Garret's head. "You don't invite a guy up to your room late at night and sit around half-naked, drawing pictures of him just for the aesthetic value of it."

"Mmmm," I grumbled. "He's had Judy up there, too."

"How do you know?"

"He told me. He showed me the portrait. Plus, I got up to go to the bathroom late the other night and she was coming down from the attic *again*. She *loves* that I saw her, too. Monster."

"I don't get it," Ian said. "The last I heard, you were freaked out by the fact that your dad had invited Garret to live in your house. Now he's all you can talk about. What changed, besides the fact that you're now acknowledging how cute he is? You *are*, right? Because if you aren't, I'm going to take your temperature."

Everything had changed. I couldn't perform The Great Unspoken Act without thinking about Garret. I couldn't see enough of him. I couldn't help hating Judy for spending time with him in the attic. I had a major crush, plain and simple. I was obsessed. I was—did I even know what the words meant?—in love.

Okay, that's one of my classic exaggerations. I was in like. And in lust.

Ian was still waiting for me to tell him what had changed. He watched me now for a few seconds as I gazed at Garret; then he grinned and said, "Never mind, you don't have to answer. I can see it in your eyes."

Just then, the girl sitting next to Garret got up and switched seats to talk to a friend.

"There's your chance," Ian said, nudging me. *"Go."*

"Go what?"

"Talk to him outside of the Tokyo that is your house."

He had a point. I jumped up from my seat and walked down the aisle. Boldly, without even asking, I sat down next to Garret. "How's it going?"

"Fine. Yourself?"

"Myself is doing grand," I said. "Excited about the trip?"

"It's great not to be in class, but I'm dreading it, I must confess."

"Why?"

"Because..." Garret glanced out the bus window at the trees racing by. "...this is going to be people walking around in costumes, right? Bonnets and three-cornered hats? Pretending we're back in the seventeen hundreds?"

"Pretty much."

"I hate that sort of thing. I find it so...banal."

Another word I'd have to look up. "Well, next year we get to go to Kings Dominion."

"Next year *you* get to go to Kings Dominion. I'll be living in San Diego. If we haven't moved again by then."

What a stupid slip of the tongue. How could I have forgotten, even for a moment, that he was about to move away? Suddenly, the thought depressed me.

"Another Dylan shirt," he observed.

I glanced down. I was wearing a shirt I'd gotten at a Wolf Trap concert the previous year. "Yeah. It was fun, seeing him live. He changes his songs around so much, and sings them so fast, he's halfway through one of them before you know which one it is."

"And you play guitar?"

I nodded.

"I've heard you playing sometimes from the hallway," he said. "You're pretty good."

"Thanks." It was the first time anyone had ever said anything positive about my playing. Tommy, Dexter, and especially Judy all called it noise.

"Maybe you could play for me before I leave," he said.

Again, the leaving issue. "You don't hate the performance thing, too? You don't find it...banal?" I was trying to lighten the mood—just a little bit.

"I find almost *everything* banal," he said, and let out a little laugh. Then he looked me in the eye. "But not the idea of hearing you play. I wouldn't have suggested it if I did."

I thought I was going to...you know...*boing!* right there on the spot, but then he added:

"Do you think Judy would want to be in the audience?"

Judy. The anti-boing. "I think her religion prevents it," I said flatly.

"Oh, she's faking that whole religious thing."

"She *admitted* it?"

"Shhh." He tapped my hand. "She did. She thought it would help us bond, I guess. But don't tell her I told you."

"Did it?"

"Did it what?"

"Help you bond."

He looked forward, a ponderous expression on his face, as if deciding. I didn't want to hear the answer if it was yes.

Before he could speak, Judy plopped down onto the seat directly behind us, just vacated by another student. With a little too much enthusiasm, she said, "Hi, boys!"

"Hi," Garret said.

I glared at her.

"Kyle," she said, "Sasha wants to ask you something."

"She does not."

"She does. Seriously. She thinks her cousin might be gay and wants to ask you."

I glanced down the length of the bus. Sasha waved at me.

"What does she think, I have a list of names?"

"Just talk to her, will you?"

I sighed, got up, and walked down the aisle. Sasha was smiling broadly. "Well?" I asked, sitting next to her.

"Well, what?"

"Judy said you might have a gay cousin or something?"

Sasha shrieked and the sound echoed off the bus windows. "I wondered what she was going to come up with to get you back here. I don't even *have* a cousin! Not that I'd care if I had a gay one, or anything. I mean, gay people are all right with me!"

I looked forward, and of course Judy was now sitting where I'd been, next to Garret. Between them and us, I saw Ian looking wide-eyed, his thumb jerking toward my monster sister and my vampire crush. I bugged my own eyes out and shrugged at him.

Ferris Coover moved up a row so that he was sitting directly across from me. He stared at me until I said, "How's the book coming along?"

"You're not going to do anything about this situation, are you?"

"What situation?"

"Garret Johnson is talking to your sister right now."

"So?"

"He could turn her into one of them in a heartbeat."

"It might be an improvement."

"I'm the only one who cares," Coover said, shaking his head.

"I care!" Sasha proclaimed. "About what?"

I ignored her and told Coover, "If 'caring' means throwing water on somebody in a food court, then I'd rather not 'care.' You're lucky mall security didn't come after you."

"I thought the Lourdes water would work. I was wrong. But there are other ways. You'll thank me, in the end."

"You're scaring me," I said, trying to make it sound sarcastic even though, in truth, he *was* scaring me a little. He looked dead serious.

His eyes shifted around, taking in the students, the bus, the world going past the windows. After a moment he said, "Isn't it strange that these buses don't have seat belts? They show us those driver's ed films where people get mutilated because they aren't wearing their seat belts, and yet if something slammed into this bus right now and it flipped over, we'd be like meat in a blender."

I didn't know what to say to that. Sasha looked horrified and afraid to speak.

I got up and walked back to the empty seat behind Garret and Judy.

"How's Sasha's gay cousin?" she asked.

"Turns out he's not gay. He just likes having his eyebrows threaded. Listen, I don't know why I'm telling you this because I don't really care, but Ferris Coover is going through your purse right now."

"Damn that little freak!" she snapped, then got up and practically ran down the aisle to the back of the bus.

I sat back down beside Garret. He grinned at me. "He isn't, is he?"

"He's a vampire hunter, not a thief," I said.

"I don't know why you and your sister can't get along." He was still smiling, and it occurred to me for the first time: He didn't seem at all bothered by the fact that we didn't get along. He seemed to *like* it.

It was a clear, hot day—not ideal for walking around a town with almost no shade. We were lined up in five alphabetical groups (which put me and Judy together, of course, and Garret in the group closer to the middle of the alphabet, with Ian— who, I'm sure, appreciated the view). For the first half of the day we had to travel within our group and do group things, like tour the Governor's Palace (a virtual arsenal of rifles when you first walked in—even more so than the magazine where all the munitions were supposed to be stored), attend a Fifes and Drums performance (oh, boy), get lectured on colonial gardening techniques (yawn), and walk alongside a man dressed up like George Washington as he marched from the Capitol to the Courthouse so that he could pretend to start the Revolutionary War. I don't mean to make it sound deadly; some of it was pretty interesting, like the guy who was an old-fashioned wheelwright was actually making wheels, and the saddler was making saddles, and the butter-maker was making butter. Somehow, the parts that involved making things were more impressive to me than a guy walking around pretending to be George Washington or Patrick Henry. And as for the other "performers," I remembered what Garret had said and I still had to look up *banal*, but I thought the whole idea of these people milling about in period costumes, as if we'd all traveled back in time, was as cornball as could be. I mean, *every*body was smiling. *Happy to be here* (back when dentists yanked your teeth without anesthesia)! *Couldn't be more delighted* (though the first thing you saw, whenever you traveled by carriage, was the ass-end of a horse taking a poop)! *Top of the morning to you* (oh, and by the way— you're a slave)!

Through it all, Judy and I didn't say a word to each other. As our group made its way from one attraction to another, we occasionally passed the other groups from our school, and we were both keeping an eye out for Garret. A "militia sergeant" conducted a drill. A "rifleman" loaded and fired a musket. A "town crier" announced a public debate about the "brand-new" Declaration of Independence. But there was no sign of Garret.

The second half of the day was a free-for-all. That is, we got to do whatever we wanted. Judy and Sasha took a carriage ride around town. I found Ian in a candy shop in the market area watching them make old-fashioned taffy (which he paid for, I noticed, with up-to-date money).

"Want some?" he asked around a mouthful, holding open the bag.

"No, thanks. Taffy's not my thing."

"Taffy is me," he said. "I am taffy. How's the day going so far?"

"Okay, I guess. It's like the past, if everyone was on massive amounts of antidepressants."

"Yeah, if I had one of these jobs, walking around all dressed up, I'd be smiling big-time, but in my head I'd be singing, *Go to hell, go to hell, go to hell....*"

I laughed. "I always thought if I worked at Kings Dominion and wore one of those big animal costumes, I'd be having my picture taken with all these kids, and in every picture I'd be waving my paw, but *really* I'd be shooting everyone the bird and no one would ever know."

"I'd say that's sick, but it seems to work on the same principle as the 'Go to Hell' song."

"Have you seen Garret?"

"He disappeared. Like, he was there at the Fifes and Drums performance, and then he was gone, and the chaperone didn't even seem to notice. I wish I was that gutsy. I guess he's not too worried about getting in trouble, since he's not going to be around much longer."

"Don't remind me."

"Ouch. Sorry. At least you know he wasn't running around with your sister. She was in your group."

"Such a charmer, that one. She and Sasha are taking a horse-poop tour around town as we speak."

"Want me to help you look for Garret?"

"Nah. But if you spot Coover, keep an eye on him. He seems more on the warpath than ever."

"I don't think 'warpath' is politically correct anymore but— will do."

I took a piece of taffy after all, and then walked around

trying to pry it from my teeth with my tongue while I searched for Garret.

I was walking through the gardens behind the Capitol building when I spotted him entering the hedge maze. The hedges didn't grow up high enough to swallow him; I could see his shoulders and head moving around in that sea of green, so I entered, too, and tried to catch up with him.

The maze was harder than it looked. I kept taking wrong turns, and he kept getting farther away. He saw me a couple of times as he wandered, I thought, but I wasn't sure. There was another head sticking out of the maze: Sasha's. That meant Judy couldn't be far behind—and sure enough, there she was… closer to Garret than I was. I started walking faster, and continued to take wrong turns, cursing under my breath, sweating in the hot sun, my Dylan T-shirt sticking to my chest. When I was finally gaining on him, I saw that Sasha was rows away but Judy was right there, facing him. They were talking, but they were too far away for me to hear what they were saying. *What now?* I wondered, because I wasn't crazy about the idea of the three of us all bunched up on top of one another in the middle of a hedge maze. But I kept moving. I was rounding the corner to where they stood when I heard him laugh and say, "Okay, whatever." Then he leaned forward and gave her a quick peck on the lips. Well, not so quick. I don't know if there was any tongue action or not, but the kiss lasted a few seconds.

I was embarrassed by my anger. Still, I barreled toward them.

"What are you guys doing?" I asked, unable to restrain myself.

Garret pulled back. Judy looked over at me and said, "What are *you* doing, *stalking* us?"

"I'm seeing the sights," I said. "I'm checking out the maze."

"Us, too," Judy said, smiling.

I wanted to smack her. I'm sure they could both see how mad I was.

Garret sighed and said, "I was just telling your sister how bored I am. I've been wandering around this ridiculous town for hours, killing time with both hands."

"Apparently," I said, glaring at Judy. I turned and walked away—and of course it took about ten minutes to find my way out of that stupid hedge.

For a while, I just sat under an eave of one of those old buildings and watched them. They didn't kiss again. Whether or not they were holding hands, I couldn't tell because of the hedge. Just as they were finally reemerging, Ferris Coover came walking toward them with both hands raised, holding something.

A gun.

A *musket*.

How he'd gotten it, I have no idea; maybe he'd swiped it from the cart the rifleman had hauled out. He was shouting, "Death to evil," and aiming the big clunky thing, which surely didn't work or at least wasn't loaded, but still he was aiming it at Garret as he marched forward, and both Garret and Judy were ducking to the ground.

On Coover's heels, already, were two security guards. The funny thing (if there can be anything funny about somebody waving a gun at somebody else) is that the guards were dressed in period costumes. They looked like constables, or old-time sheriffs. But they weren't actors. They grabbed him by the shoulders and took the gun away, then dragged him off to the security office.

On the ride back to the school, there was a lot less moving around (everyone was tired and baked from the heat). Coover wasn't on our bus, or on any of the other buses. He was being held at Colonial Williamsburg until his parents came and got him. There was already talk that he was going to be suspended for his gun stunt.

I sat next to Ian but refused to tell him why I was in a bad mood. He probably assumed it was because I was mad at Coover for potentially putting Garret's life in danger. But it wasn't that. Ian—the only kid besides me on the bus *not* talking about Coover and the musket—yammered on about his crush on some *American Idol* singer and how he was the hottest person to ever be on the show. I ignored him, and finally he got up and said, "Think I'll go find someone to sit next to who has a pulse," and switched seats.

Almost immediately, Judy plopped down where he'd been sitting.

"So," she said, "about Garret."

"I wish you'd taken the musket ball."

"Please. It turns out it wasn't even a real gun, though apparently Coover didn't know that. Anyway, I just want you to know: You won't have Garret. You can't. He isn't gay."

"Uh-huh. And you're religious."

"Just because I kiss a boy doesn't mean I can't be religious."

"You're *faking* it," I told her. "You've been faking the whole time, just to try to date Jacob. And now that he knows you're a big fat phony and wants nothing to do with you, you're going after Garret, only because you know I like him. Garret told me all about it."

The "big fat" part was mean. Judy wasn't fat, but I knew she thought she was. I saw the sting of the remark register on her face. Then a different sting registered. "Wait, Garret *told* you?"

"Yeah. Was he not supposed to?" I sneered.

She had a piece of gum in her mouth (maybe it was that awful taffy). She narrowed her eyes at me and worked her jaw like she was powdering the bones of a small animal. Then she got up and moved to another seat.

I wanted to talk to Garret, to find out what the hell was going on, but I couldn't even look at him. Plus, given what had just happened with Coover, I had no idea if Garret was shaken up or not, and I felt a little silly being bent out of shape about his kissing my sister, given what else had occurred that day.

Dinner was a great big war of words, though Garret and Judy and I kept pretty silent. There was a lot of talk about the Coover incident (no one but Garret, Judy, and me seemed to know it had anything to do with Garret's claim to be a vampire). Judy kept her eye on me a lot, which was irritating to no end. We were both on cleanup detail, and as I was loading the dishwasher, she clacked a stack of plates onto the counter and said under her breath, "I despise you."

"I despise you back," I whispered. Mom and Dad were still in the dining room, just out of earshot.

"I despise you *forever*," she hissed.

I kept thinking about Garret and waiting for her to say the words *I win*, but she never did, which was even worse than if she'd said them, because it made me realize she didn't have to.

8. JUDY:
A glutton for punishment,
one zinger at a time

Sasha came over the evening after Junior Jaunt and we sat in my room, on my bed, studying for our upcoming science test. *Pretending* to study is a more accurate way of putting it. I would read one of the practice questions from the sheet Mr. Wintall had given us, Sasha would offer up some lame excuse for an answer, then we would talk about something else.

" 'Describe the big bang theory,' " I read to her from the practice sheet.

She balled her fists together, said, "Bang!" and thrust her hands outward.

"Theory," I said. "Describe the *theory.*"

"Everything in the universe was packed together really tight, like the inside of a golf ball—have you ever seen what's in there? It's a million rubber bands all jammed together."

"I think you missed a few steps. 'What was formed a second after the big bang?'"

"Hey, the big bang is like your house! A ton of people all crammed together, and one day it's going to explode!"

"The answer is gravity," I said. "Gravity was formed a second after the big bang."

"Lucky for us. Hey, do you think they'll really suspend Coover?"

"Hello? He aimed a *musket* at me. Well, at Garret, but I was definitely in the line of fire."

"That's so antisocial, don't you think? I mean, that guy needs counseling."

"'Provide a brief explanation of Einstein's theory of relativity.'"

"It's all relative," Sasha said.

"Maybe they *won't* suspend him, though. It's not like he tried to shoot us on school grounds."

"Yeah, but it was a field trip," she said. "It was a school function."

"Who knows."

"Is Garret freaked out?"

"I haven't talked to him since we got back."

"No? You haven't talked to Jacob lately, either. What's up with that?"

Sasha didn't know about the kiss in the hedge maze. She also didn't know about my running out of the church. Or Garret's ratting me out to Kyle. I just didn't feel like answering a thousand questions about what it all *meant*, and where it was all *going*. "Have you studied at all, before today?" I asked her. "This test is going to be huge, you know."

"I couldn't. I'm not like you; I can't just sit down by myself and *study*." She made air quotes around *study*, like it was a myth invented to wreck her life. "You're probably ready to ace the test, aren't you?"

"Try me," I said, and handed her the practice questions. "Ask me something."

She scanned her eyes over the page. " 'Who employed an apple to advance the field of cosmology?' "

"That's easy. Jimmy Neutron."

She started reading the next question.

"Sasha!" I said. "Jimmy Neutron is that kid in the cartoons! The correct answer is Isaac Newton."

"You might get half-credit for that, though. The names are similar. So are you really not going to go to bible study this Saturday?"

I'd told her I'd be free just in case there was something to do that she knew about; now I wished I'd just kept my mouth shut. "I don't want to talk about it."

"Is it because of the Barbie girl? What's her name...Tina?"

I flopped down flat on my back and let my head hang over the edge of the mattress, so that everything in sight— the floor, my dresser, the picture of Jesus—was upside down.

"Did you ever think about studying English as a second language?"

"Huh?"

"I. Don't. Want. To. Talk about it!"

"You're confusing me. Hey, speaking of which, what do you want to be?"

The blood was already rushing to my head. I sat up and looked at her. "Tell me you don't mean, 'when I grow up.'"

"Yeah. When you grow up, what do you want to be?"

"Who cares? I've got more important things to think about at the moment."

"Well, don't you think you should have *some* sort of idea? I mean, isn't it scary that you don't know at all?"

"You sound like my mom talking to Dexter."

"I wanted to be a meteorologist, but then I found out it has nothing to do with meteors."

"Come on," I said. "*You* have an interest in meteors?"

"Think how easy it would be if your job was observing meteors. There's hardly ever one! Halley's Comet comes around every hundred years or something. And when they have those meteor showers, they're over within, like, five seconds. You'd hardly have any work to do! Anyway, I found out it's just a fancy name for the weatherman. And I don't think there *are* any weather women. Have you ever seen one?"

"That's no reason not to try, if you're interested."

"Weather's boring."

"And just so you know? Taxidermy's got nothing to do with taxes, either. Or taxis."

"I know *that*," she said.

"And horticulture has nothing to do with whores."

She flung a pillow at me. "Shut up! You must have *some* idea what you want to do. We'll be applying to colleges next year. Don't they make you declare a major?"

"I know for a fact, from Tommy, that you can change your major as many times as you want during the first couple of years."

"Maybe you could major in major-changing," Sasha said, and snorted at herself. "Really, though, if you had to pick one— doctor, lawyer, waitress—what would it be?"

"Why are you asking me this?" I snatched the practice questions out of her hand for no reason.

"I just worry about you, that's all."

What? Not that I'd ever given it any thought, but no one my own age (or even close to it) had ever expressed any sort of *worry* for me. The fact that Sasha—far from the brightest bulb—was worried about me was downright disturbing.

"Why in the world are you worried about *me*?" I asked.

"You just seem to be getting all...fuzzy...lately."

"Fuzzy how?"

"First, you're not interested in dating anyone, then you're hot for that painter guy, Sean, so suddenly you're a 'painter.'"

(I'd forgotten about that. It had happened last year, after all.)

"Then you've got a crush on Brent Hartley, so for five

minutes you're this big 'tennis player,' carrying a racket around even though you don't know how to play."

(I'd forgotten about that one, too.)

"Then Jacob comes along and suddenly you're 'born-again.'"

"I never claimed to be born-again. I told him I was considering it. And I was pretending; you know that. It was just to get him to like me."

"I know, but see what I mean? You're all fuzzy. And you don't have any hobbies or ever talk about what you want to *do* with your life."

"Who are you, my guidance counselor?"

"No, I'm your friend. But what's next? I keep waiting for you to tell me you're going to start pretending to be a vampire to get Garret to like you."

"I told you I don't want to talk about Garret. *Or* Jacob."

"I'm *not* talking about them. I'm talking about *you*. I just worry that you're going to disappear if you keep pretending to be stuff you're not!"

"You know what?" I said. "I don't feel like being life-coached by a ditz, okay? I just don't think I need that right now. You didn't even know what meteorology was! You're the biggest airhead I've ever known!" I crumpled up the practice question sheet and tossed it into her lap. "I think I'm done studying for the night. Happy failing."

Her face had darkened, listening to my tirade. I couldn't stop; it just poured out of me, like lava from a volcano. I wanted to incinerate her. Then, instantly, I wanted to take it all back.

"You're always talking down to me," she said quietly.

"No, I'm not," I said. "Never mind what I said, okay? Forget about it." I could tell she was seriously upset, and it was scaring me. Her eyes were glassing over.

"I keep waiting for you to stop doing it, because you're my friend. But I don't think you're ever going to stop. You're just... mean. From the inside out." She was crying now, but without making any crying sounds.

"Sasha, look, I'm just in a really bad mood."

She shook her head no. "I'm going home. I'm through."

"Through what?"

"Waiting for you to be nice." She got up from the bed and gathered her books and her purse.

"Sasha, wait!"

"See you around," she said.

"Listen, I'm... I'm..." Why was it so hard to say? "I'm sorry!"

But she walked out of the room, still shaking her head. And what felt like the worst part of all, for some reason: She uncrumpled the sheet of practice questions, folded it, and tucked it into her pocket as she left.

I sat there for a while, trying to figure out who I was more angry with: myself, or everyone else. The answer was obvious—and didn't feel good. It also didn't fix anything. But I wasn't much in the mood to fix things.

I climbed the stairs to the attic and pounded on the door.

"Who is it?"

"Judy," I said. "I want to talk to you."

"I'm doing my homework right now," Garret called through the door.

I'd never heard that from him before. "It's my house. Open up."

He waited a few moments. I was on the verge of trying the handle when I heard him unlock the door. It swung open.

"Do you use that line on your siblings, too? 'It's my house. Open up'?"

"Never tried it. But I see enough of them as it is; I don't usually go knocking on doors."

"I should be flattered, then."

"Whatever. Be flattered. I don't care."

"You sound upset."

"No, I don't." I walked past him into the game room. There were no schoolbooks open that I could see. No papers out. "You lied. You weren't doing homework."

"You're right; I just felt like being alone. But make yourself at home."

I closed the door behind me and stood next to it. He walked back over to his bed, where his sketch pad lay open alongside his box of charcoals. Then he sat down, pulled the pad onto his lap, and selected a piece of charcoal from the box. "Recovered from yesterday's events?" he asked, looking at me and beginning to draw.

"Don't draw me. I'm mad at you."

"Why?"

"What are you up to, anyway? I mean, what's your game?"

"I don't have a 'game.'"

"Bull. You put on this act, pretending to be something you're not, and you play with people's heads."

"Funny. That sounds like a description of you." He was still drawing. He made a few more lines, flipped the page, and started again, eyeballing me.

"Why did you tell Kyle about my religious thing?"

"You mean, your *pretending* to be religious?"

"Yeah, that. I told you that was a secret."

"I guess it slipped out," he said.

"Yeah? Well, I don't believe that. You're not a very trustworthy person, you know?"

"Not true. But even if it were, what motivation would I have to be *trustworthy*? I'll be gone in a week. I'll never see any of you again."

"Stop *drawing* me," I said. It was like having someone stick a camera in my face and click away.

He didn't stop. He was working fast, and was on his third page.

"You should be trustworthy because it's the right thing to do," I said.

"You're a curious one to be giving moral advice," he said. "You actually *sound* religious, for once. It doesn't count for much, though, coming from you."

"What's that supposed to mean?"

"You're pretty vicious with people, aren't you? Even your own brother. Your *twin*."

What was this, Bash Judy Night? Had he been listening through the air-conditioning vent to my conversation with Sasha? "My behavior toward my brother—or anyone else—has got nothing to do with you. You couldn't matter less to me."

"No? So tell me, then, why did you ask me to kiss you when we were in the hedge maze?"

He was right about that much; I *had* asked him to kiss me. But he'd done it, so fair was fair, right? Actually, the way the night was going, I wasn't sure what "right" was anymore. "Look, if you didn't want to kiss me, you should have just told me no."

"Correct," he said, finishing the third unwelcome drawing. He dropped the charcoal stick back into the box. "I didn't tell you no because I wanted to do it."

"You did?"

"Let's just say I had my reasons."

"Well, I had mine, too."

The bleating of his cell phone erupted from his backpack on the floor beside his bed. In the past, he'd appeared to welcome these calls. Now he groaned, seemed to reluctantly reach for the backpack, and dug out the phone. "Sorry," he said to me. And then, "Hello?"

I stayed by the door with my arms across my stomach.

"Yes," he said into the phone. And then, "*Yes*, I'm doing my best. But these mortals can be difficult. Some of them are a little...unsettled...having one of our kind in their home." He glanced at me as he said this. "I'll sink my teeth into one of them soon, I promise....I said I *promise*, okay? I have to go....You, too. Goodnight." He folded the phone up and dropped it into the backpack.

"Helena?"

"Yes, that was Helena."

"You're so *fake*," I said, wishing I'd never come upstairs. "You move into our house, behave like a total weirdo, and expect us all to just...accept it."

"Judy," he said, reclining now on the bed in such a relaxed manner, compared to my own jitteriness, that I wanted to strangle him, "what exactly are you here to tell me?"

"That I'm mad at you! That you shouldn't have ratted me out to Kyle! That you just use people for your own amusement!" Suddenly, I thought of something else. "I *also* came up to tell you that the only reason I asked you to kiss me was that I knew Kyle was standing just a few feet away, and I wanted to make him jealous."

I realized as I said this that I was only confirming his accusation that I wasn't nice to Kyle, but I didn't care. At that point, I was trying to say anything that might wound him in some way.

But he came back with a zinger. "Well, that makes two of us."

"Meaning what?"

"I knew he was there, too," Garret said. "Looks like you and I kissed for the same reason."

My head was swimming. I couldn't piece it all together, and didn't want to anymore. One thing was clear: Just like with Sasha, I wasn't going to come out a winner in this situation. I said, "You should just drop the stupid vampire thing. It's obviously an act."

"Is it?" Garret asked, and then smiled at me, showing teeth. I have to admit, his incisors did look a little long.

I pulled the door open and stomped back down the stairs.

Was there any final act of humiliation I had left to commit that night? Yes, there was one. I sat on my bed and dialed Jacob's number.

I know, I know—I'm a glutton for punishment, right? But I felt doors closing all around me, and wanted to see if at least *one* of them was still open—even if by a few inches.

His dad answered. Again, he hollered for Jacob without lowering the phone. I heard Jacob in the distance ask, "Who is it?" and right into the receiver his dad said, "Some girl. Doesn't sound like Tina."

It was the closest thing I'd had to a compliment all day.

A moment later, Jacob got on the line. "Hello?"

"Hi. It's Judy."

"Oh. I was wondering if you were going to call."

"Yeah. Well. Listen, about last Sunday..."

My pause was deliberate. I wanted to give him a chance to say *Don't worry about it,* or *Oh, forget it — everyone gets stage fright.* But all he said was, "Yeah?"

What else did I have to lose, at that point? "I want to totally come clean with you. I wasn't...what I mean is, I haven't been...I'm not very religious."

"I know that," he said flatly.

"You do?"

"I kind of figured it out when you ran out of the church. But I knew before that, too. It's always been obvious you don't care about what goes on in study."

"I care. About seeing you, I mean. I just wasn't up front about my main reason for being there. Well, my *only* reason. Can't you just take that as a compliment?"

"Sure," he said. "I take it as a compliment. But it's a little insulting, too."

"Why is it insulting?"

"You were basically making fun of everyone in the group, including me, by acting like you shared our beliefs when you didn't."

"Well, I didn't mean to *insult* anyone."

"And you were abusive to Tina."

"Tina? She hasn't exactly been Miss Congeniality, you know."

He sighed into the phone. "Maybe you just bring out the worst in people."

Jesus! (Good thing I thought that, as opposed to saying it out loud.) "Look, I'm telling you I'm sorry, okay? I'm apologizing for pretending to be something I wasn't."

"Fine."

"*Is* it fine? I mean, can we still…hang out? Not at study, of course, and not around Tina. And I don't mean 'hang out' in any *date* kind of way. I just mean, be friends."

"I don't think that's a good idea."

"Wait—aren't you supposed to be forgiving? Isn't it the Christian thing to do? Hate the sin, not the sinner?"

"I do forgive you. And I don't hate you. I just don't like you very much."

I didn't know whether to hang up, start yelling, or cry. I sort of felt like doing all three.

"You broke a bond of trust, Judy. Once that's broken, it's not really possible to have a friendship. With me, anyway."

I felt my eyes go damp, and my mouth began to quiver. I hated him and loved him, and for some awful reason it felt now like we actually *had* dated for a while, and that he was breaking up with me. "Why don't you just condemn me to hell?!" I yelled, and then hit the button, ending the call.

Not exactly the best night of my life. The worst, in fact. Do you know what it's like to absolutely, positively, and wholeheartedly hate yourself? Let me say something nice (for a change): I hope not.

9. K Y L E :
Twenty questions,
but really just one

For the next week, I was the Lone Ranger of the Renneker house. That is, I kept to myself whenever I could: in my room, with the door shut and locked. I even faked having a stomachache at dinnertime for a few nights so that I wouldn't have to see anyone. I *heard* them, of course, because our house was a constant symphony of voices and thumps, feet on the stairs, Rollerblade races in the hallways, the drone of the television, and the hum of the automatic garage door. But I pretended I was invisible most of the time, and I said as little as possible to anyone who spoke to me. I studied for my upcoming finals, played my guitar, and fought off the urge to ask Garret what was going on.

The third night in a row that I missed dinner, there was a knock at my door. "Kyle? It's your dad. May I come in?"

I got up from my desk, unlocked the door, and opened it. He was holding a plate of food and was poised like a waiter in a fancy restaurant, his back straight and his belly stuck out, his head tilted back slightly so that he was looking at me down the bridge of his nose, through his glasses. A cloth napkin hung from his arm. "Your dinner, sir."

"Wow. Thanks," I said. True, I wanted to be alone, but true, also, I was hungry.

Instead of the ballpoint pen that was usually sticking out of his shirt pocket, he had a fork and knife. "Tonight's special is meat loaf, broccoli, and mashed potatoes. Will that sit okay with your stomach?"

"Sure," I said. "I mean, probably." I cleared my books away and he set the plate down on the desk, along with the fork and the knife.

"Let's feel your forehead." He held his palm against my head for a moment. "No fever, it seems. Any aches or pains?"

"Just my stomach," I lied. "A little achy."

"Maybe something's just not agreeing with you."

That's for sure.

He sat down on the edge of my bed and casually sifted through my schoolbooks while I ate.

"Advanced Geometry for High School Students," he read off one of the covers. "I wonder why they never give textbooks more dynamic names to make them more appealing."

"Like what?" I said around a mouthful of meat loaf.

"Oh, I don't know. *Geometry—Wow!*"

"Sounds like a page-turner."

"I have to admit, geometry was the only math course I ever had any interest in. Or did very well in, for that matter. So, Kyle." He crossed one leg over the other, took off his glasses, and held them by one stem in the same hand he rested his chin on. "Do you mind if I ask you something potentially intrusive?"

"Are you clicking into shrink mode?"

"I am. It's obvious, right? I'm an open book, as they say. Which is not always the best thing to be, but in this case I believe it serves us both well."

Dad and his presentations. His way with words. He was one in a million, that was for sure. "Okay," I said hesitantly, "shoot."

"You've been spending a lot of time in your room lately. Normal for an adolescent boy, of course—but up to a point. The fact that you're skipping dinners now gives me concern. It means you either have no appetite, or don't want to be around other people. My natural concern is that either one of these might be a sign of mild depression. And I don't like to let these things go unchecked for very long. That's how they spiral out of control."

"Well...," I said, trying to decide how I wanted to respond.

"Here's my question: *Are* you depressed or maybe upset about something, or is this genuinely a stomachache? And please notice that I'm not trying to pry out of you *what* you're upset about, if in fact you are."

He must be an effective shrink. He has this direct, mock-formal manner—and I found it impossible to lie to him. "My stomach's fine," I said. "Sorry I lied about that. I hope you're not mad."

"I'm not. I'm relieved, in fact, because if it *was* your stomach, a trip to the doctor would be the next step, after three days of pain, and I'd have to be the one to take you to the doctor tomorrow because your mother's day is eaten up with errands." He winked at me. "But it means something else is going on with you. Is that right?"

"Right."

"Something of an emotional nature?"

I nodded and stuffed a piece of broccoli into my mouth.

"Would you say it's something minor, or titanic?"

"In the middle."

"Aha. And does it feel like something temporary, or long-lasting?"

"Temporary. But maybe not."

"Concerning just you, or yourself and others?"

"Me and a couple of other people."

"Something of a romantic nature, perhaps?"

I winced. "Sort of."

"And do you feel in control, *somewhat* in control, or *completely* out of control of the situation?"

Maybe he wasn't such a good shrink, after all. Was this the way he always tackled patients? By playing twenty questions?

"I feel pretty much out of control. I mean, I can't control it, or change it. I don't think so, anyway. Don't you want to just ask me what it is?"

"No, no. I respect your privacy. If you want to tell me, you will. At this point, I just want to check in and test the waters, so to speak. Give you the opportunity to solicit advice, should you want it. And try to get a read on your emotional well-being. I know the flock is enormous, but I don't like it when one of them goes off alone with a problem and hides for very long."

"What do you do when something you don't like happens and you have no control over it—I mean *none*?" I asked.

He raised his brow and thought for a moment. "I accept it."

Easier said than done. *Psychology needs to be a little more functional,* I thought. "So what's the read on my 'emotional well-being'?"

"You seem a little sad. A little distracted. A little agitated, maybe."

Check. Check. Check.

"You don't seem desperate, or in heavy despair, which is good. But these things don't always reside on the surface. Just because I don't see them doesn't mean they aren't there."

"I'm dealing with it, Dad."

"Are you? Well, that's good. If you want to talk to somebody, I'm here. Or if you want to talk to somebody else, that can be arranged, too. Your problems are never bigger than you are, Kyle. It's a geometric impossibility. Though sometimes it may feel like they're larger than an elephant. Okay?"

I thanked him again for bringing me dinner. He got up from the bed and said, "We're having red velvet cake for dessert, and that's the carrot I'll dangle before you. If you want a piece, you'll have to come downstairs to get it. Fair enough?"

"Sure," I said. No red velvet cake for me.

"All right, then. Enjoy the rest of your meal. I'm glad we had this talk." He patted me on the back, walked out of the room, and closed the door behind him.

Avoiding Garret at school proved to be even tougher than avoiding him in my house, since we shared two classes. But still I managed not to talk to him. There was one afternoon in gym when we were all out on the field playing flag football, and as we were finishing up and heading back to the locker room, I saw him out of the corner of my eye, walking in my direction, *maybe* intending to speak to me. But I veered away and fast-stepped it inside. I thought, *If I can just stay in this holding pattern until he leaves, I won't ever have to hear from him about how he's into Judy, not me, and once he's gone, Judy won't have him, either.*

Of course, I had no idea if she and Garret were hanging out together. I told myself I didn't care, but I did. At night, I lay in bed and listened to the ceiling to see if I could detect two sets of footsteps instead of one.

Somehow, distracted as I was, I did fine on all my tests. Better than fine on some of them. Most of my teachers scheduled their final tests for the second-to-last week of school so that they could get our grades to us in time, which made the last week a very laid-back affair. Just what I needed: even more time to think.

My calculus teacher, Mr. Hedleston, decided to get up close and personal with us in those last five days of class. He, who'd been a ballbuster all year, who'd hardly ever cracked a smile, leaned back against his desk with his hands in his pockets and told us stories about his long and distinguished teaching career, about how he'd taught all sorts of math, and about how his students had gone on to do some amazing things (one was now a partner at a big corporate New York law firm—woo-hoo!). "Okay," he said, smacking his hands together, finally done with his list of achievements. "Let's open up the floor."

We're supposed to talk about ourselves now? I wondered.

But he said, "I want you to ask me anything you want to know about math. It doesn't have to be calculus. It can be any kind of math at all. You ask, and I'll answer."

Crickets. The rustling of a tumbleweed.

Ian, who sat behind me, tapped my shoulder and passed me a note. I unfolded it in my lap. It read:

CAN'T THINK. GETTING DIZZY.
BLOOD IS DRIPPING FROM MY EARS.

And below that:

DID YOU HEAR ABOUT COOVER?

I had to wait till class was over to find out the news about Coover, though at that point, I couldn't have cared less. Ian was waiting for me in the hall.

"Wow," he said when I came out. "Pure death."

"Coover's dead?"

"No, that *class*. I thought he'd *never* stop talking!"

"Well, the school year's almost over. We won't have to hear old man Hedleston anymore."

"Unless we get him next year for trig. 'Ask me anything you want to know about *math*'? Please!"

We both had our next classes in D wing, so we headed that way. "What's the news on Coover?" I asked. "Did he get suspended?"

"*Beyond* suspended. He's not finishing the school year. I talked to Barry Fleck, whose mother is friends with Mrs. Coover, and word is, Coover got into serious trouble with the school, his parents, and his doctor for that Williamsburg stunt."

"His *doctor*?"

"Apparently there was a medication he was supposed to be taking, but he'd stopped."

"What, like, Ritalin?"

"Something to make him focus, or something to make him *not* focus is probably more like it. Anyway, he's on a big 'time-out' against his will while he gets his act together."

"Is he in the hospital or something?"

"No, he's at home taking it easy — if that's even possible for someone like him. So, did that whole musket thing completely piss Garret off?"

"I don't know."

"You haven't talked to him?"

"I'm not really...interacting...with Garret right now."

"Uh-oh. Is this the same situation that turned you into Mr. Grouchy on the bus ride home?"

"Yeah."

Ian held up both hands, one of them clutching his books. "Subject dropped. I don't like the grouchy you. It's too close to the grouchy *me*."

"I'm not grouchy," I said.

"Maybe we should get you some of Coover's medication."

"That isn't funny."

"Or a musket."

I tried my best to glare at him, though part of me wanted to laugh—the first time I'd had *that* impulse in a week. Leave it to Ian.

He held his hands up again. "Subject dropped," he repeated. "I dropped it—look, there it goes, rolling across the floor."

"Oh, I forgot to tell you: I outed you to my mom."

"What did she say?"

"She said she had no idea. Then she suggested we date."

"Ha! Don't take this the wrong way, but I don't think so."

"Me, either," I said. "Remember that time we tried to kiss?"

"We didn't *try*. We actually did it. That was the most boring minute of my life. Talk about lack of chemistry."

"That was a minute? I thought it was a whole day!"

"Bitch!" Ian snapped.

I did laugh then, and Ian laughed, too, and said, "Later," as he peeled off into his classroom. Alone, I remembered how amazing it had been to kiss Brent Hartley, and how amazing it *might* have been to kiss Garret, and how I wasn't going to find out, and how Judy already had.

Suddenly, nothing seemed particularly funny.

But who can predict human—or, in this case, potentially inhuman—behavior? Not me. Wouldn't try if you paid me. Wouldn't take a million dollars to predict what a particular series of events might lead to, how x might cause y only after it brushes up against w....

Well, okay, for a million dollars, I'd give it a shot, but I never saw *this* one coming:

Two days before Dexter's graduation ceremony, I was in my room playing my guitar late at night when I heard a light tapping on my door.

"Who is it?"

Something was uttered that I couldn't make out. I got up, walked over to the door, and said, "Who?"

"*Me,*" a voice hissed.

I unlocked the knob and pulled the door open. Garret stood there in the hallway, his sketch pad and box of charcoals under his arm. He was wearing a black T-shirt that had streaks of red silk-screened onto it like blood splatters, and a pair of dark jeans.

"What are you doing down here?" I asked. "Why aren't you in the attic?"

"May I come in? I'd like not to run into…anyone else out here."

"Anyone else like who?"

"Please?" he said, leaning into me slightly. I could smell his breath. He'd just brushed his teeth, I thought.

Whereas at one time I'd fantasized about his being in my room, I wasn't so crazy about the idea now. But I found it wasn't so easy to just turn off a crush when I wanted to. I vaguely remembered some quote I'd read in English class about the flesh being willing, even when the spirit wasn't. My flesh was in no position to be picky, I decided, so I stepped back and let him into the room.

He closed the door behind him and locked it.

"Well?" I asked.

"I'm not sure why I've become persona non grata around here all of the sudden, but I just thought…well, you know I'll be leaving before long. I'm flying out to San Diego."

"I know."

"There are two things I'd like to do before I go, if you're willing."

I swallowed nervously, but tried to look indifferent; I was tired of being nervous around him. I walked over to my bed and sat down. He took my desk chair, turning it around to face the bed. "What are they?" I asked.

"I'd like for you to play me something on your guitar. Maybe something you wrote."

My guitar was lying on the mattress next to me. "I don't write songs. I want to, but I haven't yet. I'm still learning how to play."

"Then maybe you could play me something you've learned. A Bob Dylan song."

I didn't know where this was going, and I was suspicious. Maybe he was setting me up to show me he was unimpressed. "What's the other thing?"

"I want to draw you one more time. I want a decent sketch of you I can take to San Diego with me."

"I don't get it. Why this sudden interest in me?"

The coolness and confidence that usually dominated his face dissolved into a look of disappointment. He almost looked *hurt*. Glancing down at the sketch pad in his lap, he said, "My interest in you isn't 'sudden.' "

All I could think was that, if I told him no and asked him to leave the room, I would beat myself up for maybe the next *year* wondering what might have happened if I hadn't. Then it occurred to me that, having come downstairs, he could have knocked on any of our doors (meaning he could have knocked on Judy's), but he hadn't; he'd knocked on mine.

"All right."

His expression lit up. He said, "Great. So how about the song?"

Which one? I wondered. I didn't know that many. When I started thinking about the few I'd learned how to play, they all seemed loaded in terms of their content: "Don't Think Twice, It's All Right"? (Too mean.) "Honey, Just Allow Me One More Chance"? (Too desperate—and why should I go begging, anyway?) "All I Really Want To Do"? (Next line: "Is, baby, be friends with you." Um, nope.)

Finally, I decided on "Forever Young." What better song for someone who claimed to be immortal, right?

It wasn't a hard song to play—not the way I played it, anyway. It was in two-four time and there were only four chords to strum (I didn't know any picking patterns yet), and I'd learned to merge the way Dylan did it for the demo on *Biograph* with the way he later recorded it with The Band on *Planet Waves*, in a version that I thought sounded okay. Still, my heart was racing. My hands shook as I placed the guitar on my lap in front of me. I cleared my throat and said, "I've never really played in front of anyone before."

"Well, I can't play at all, so there's no reason to worry."

"I'm not worried," I lied. Why did I feel such pressure to impress him? *Because he's really cute,* I thought, *and even if he did kiss Judy in the hedge maze, I still want him to like me.* I curled my fingers around the neck and made an awkward C, as if I didn't have the chord already memorized, and said, "Okay, here goes nothing."

Then I strummed, and started singing in a nervous voice, *"May your heart always be joyful. May your wishes all come true."* I didn't look up while I sang. I watched my left hand, the one making the chords. My fingers felt like feet that might trip down a staircase at any moment. But I didn't trip; I carried on through the three verses, right to the end of the song. One final chord — which didn't fade out like it should have but stopped abruptly because I pulled my hand away from the frets.

"That wasn't very good," I said.

But Garret was applauding. I looked up and saw him smiling as he clapped. "That was great!" he said. "You're a natural! One day you'll be on the stage, with fans screaming in the audience and groupies waiting in the wings."

"I don't think so," I said. "But thanks."

"I'm so glad I was brave enough to ask you to do that. Thank you."

"You're welcome." I could feel the heat in my face and knew I was blushing as I set the guitar aside, thankful to be done with my performance.

"I guess I could like Bob Dylan, if I tried," he said.

Before I could stop myself, the words were coming out of my mouth. "You sort of remind me of him. The way you look, I mean."

He stared at me with what seemed to be confusion, probably unsure whether I was trying to pay him a compliment or insult him.

"Back in the sixties," I clarified. "You both have the same kind of expression."

"And what expression is that?"

I reached over to the shelf beside my bed, pulled out the album cover for *Bringing It All Back Home*, and showed it to him. "I call it the *I-know-what-you're-about* expression."

He still didn't seem to get it.

"I think he's hot," I said. What the hell, right? I had nothing to lose at that point. "And I think he looks like you."

Maybe it was my imagination, but I could swear I heard one of Mr. Hedleston's tumbleweeds rolling by.

"So do you want to draw me, or what?"

"I do," he said. "But I want to show you something first."

He opened the sketch pad, flipped through a few pages, and said, "I hope this doesn't shock you."

Then he turned the pad around and displayed it for me.

On the page was a drawing of Judy.

All of Judy.

Naked.

Or, not naked, but in her underwear. I crawled forward on the mattress to get a closer look. Her face seemed to have been drawn quickly, the way he'd made his earlier portraits of me, but her body was sketched out more carefully, more fully. She was seated with her legs bent and crossed and her arms resting over her knees, and she was scowling, or trying to look pouty.

"Judy posed for you...like *that*?"

He gave a slight shrug. "I asked her if she would, and she said, 'Sure,' and the next thing I knew, she was out of her clothes and sitting on the air hockey table. She also posed for this one."

He flipped the page to show me another sketch, with her body in a slightly different position. He let me get a good, long look, then flipped the page and said, "And this."

In the third sketch, she was stretched out like a cat just waking up from a nap. I drew back and waved my hand in front of my face. "Okay," I said, "that's more of my sister than I ever need to see."

"Well, like I was saying, I don't mean to shock you. I just wanted to show them to you because I'd like to draw you the same way."

I felt like Judy was in the room with us, and I very much *didn't* want her presence there. I also didn't want to be one-upped by her yet another time. It was strange. One minute, I thought I was through competing with her for Garret's attention, and the next minute, I couldn't stand the thought of letting her "win."

Still, I said, "I don't know."

"If it makes you more comfortable, I could take off whatever clothes you take off. Artists do it all the time to make their models feel not so much on display. That's what I did with Judy."

Okay, I wanted to say. But I couldn't make myself say it.

He said, "I'll go first, to make it easier." He laid the sketch pad across his lap and, without any hesitation whatsoever, lifted his T-shirt over his head and dropped it onto the carpet beside the chair.

I steeled my nerve and took off my own shirt.

Then he stood and unbuttoned his jeans.

"This is crazy," I said.

"Not in the art world, it isn't."

I didn't know what the "art world" was. All I knew was that I was in *my* world, the world of Kyle Renneker, shirtless, with a shirtless Garret Johnson, and he was taking off his jeans. He kicked his feet out of them and stood there for a moment, wearing nothing but a pair of black boxer briefs; then he sat back down, lifted the sketch pad, and opened his box of charcoals.

I was wearing my baggy khaki shorts. I got up from the bed, unbuttoned and unzipped them, and let them fall to my ankles. Nothing on now but my Fruit of the Looms. Was I springing a boner? I was, and for as excited as I felt, I wasn't happy about it. I sat back down on the bed quickly and said, "How should I... position myself?"

"However you're most comfortable," Garret told me.

There *was* no comfortable position—not for me, like that. I sat with my legs folded up, my knees in front of my chest and my arms around my ankles, the best boner-hiding position I could think of.

If he was "springing" anything, I couldn't tell, because the sketch pad was like a wall between that part of his body and me.

He started drawing. I crammed my brain with the most awful thoughts I could muster. Puppies falling off a cliff like lemmings (somehow, puppies dying seemed a lot worse than lemmings). The penguin egg rolling away from its parents in that documentary. My dad having a stroke, my mom getting in some horrible accident, Garret himself being struck by lightning and horribly disfigured. Nothing worked. Apparently, all the tragedies life had to offer could be lobbed at me and I'd march right through them, leading the way with my dick.

"So," I said, trying to think of the least sexy thing we had in common (other than Judy), "were you at all rattled by Coover aiming a musket at you?"

His eyes went from my body to the page, from the page to my body. "Well, I have to say that *was* a bit extreme."

"I heard he's not finishing out the school year. That they're keeping him at home." I tried to picture Coover in a straitjacket, screaming through a mouth restraint, slamming his body against a padded wall. Guess what? Boing.

Garret flipped the page. He said, "Why don't you try a different position?"

"Like what?"

"Maybe unfold your legs? Sit cross-legged?"

No way. But then I figured out that I could sit that way with my hands resting in my lap, which would at least partially hide the tent in my underwear. I did that, and he half-grinned at me and said, "You have a great body."

I forced a quick, fake laugh. "No, I don't. I'm skinny. My legs are like pipe cleaners."

"You have nice legs," he said. "And nice arms. And a nice chest. You have a nice everything, from what I can see."

I was flattered, of course, and excited beyond belief. But I also felt tired of being jerked around. "I don't get it," I said. "I don't get *you*."

He paused in the middle of the second drawing. "What do you mean?"

"Are you into my sister, or are you into me?"

He shrugged. "What if I'm into both of you?"

"No way," I said, not caring if I sounded stupid. "Be bi if you want to be bi, but don't be chasing after Judy, and then chasing after me. It doesn't make any sense why you'd be into both of us, because she and I are polar opposites; we're like…"

"Chalk and cheese?"

"Huh?"

"I had a philosophy teacher from Ireland once. Ms. Finnerty. If two people were opposite, she'd say they were like chalk and cheese."

"Fine. Chalk and cheese. Night and day. Whatever. It's just… *gross*."

"Well, the two of you can't be *that* different. You're both twins, and you both agreed to pose nearly nude for me."

And that's when I realized it. I don't know why I hadn't thought of it before, but suddenly it was there in my head, an indisputable fact: Judy hadn't posed in her underwear for Garret. She hated her body. She thought she was fat. She would *never* have taken her clothes off so that he could stare at her and render her on paper. He'd drawn her head a few times and added the bodies later.

"Why do you feel like you have to lie about everything?" I asked him.

"I'm sorry?"

"Judy didn't pose for you in her underwear, did she?"

He exhaled through his nose and his bare shoulders slumped a little. Then he dropped the charcoal back into the box. "No, she didn't."

"You lied to see if you could get me to take *my* clothes off. To humiliate me. Is this a game you play with people, just to see what you can get them to do?"

"Kyle, it isn't like that."

"I don't understand *any*body—on the entire planet," I said (an exaggeration, but I was upset). "Judy fakes believing in Jesus and being a bible-thumper because she thinks it'll help her get Jacob to be her boyfriend. You fake being a vampire because—I don't know—you think it makes you more *interesting* or something. If the two of you would just be *yourselves* for ten seconds—"

"I lied about Judy having posed for those drawings because I thought it was the only way I could get you out of your clothes," he said calmly. "And I very much wanted to get you out of your clothes. Does that make sense?" He set the sketch pad aside.

It was at last plainly clear that I wasn't the only citizen of Boner City.

"Well, then, why the vampire act? Once and for all, please, explain that one."

"You think it's an act?"

"I know it is."

"You *know*?" he asked, leaning forward slightly. "Because water from Lourdes doesn't kill me? Because I have a reflection when I look in the mirror? Is that how you *know*?"

I was breathing in huffs—both excited and steamed. "If you're a vampire," I said, "prove it. And don't tell me you don't have to 'prove' anything to anybody. Prove it to *me*, right now."

It was maybe the bossiest moment of my life. I don't even know what I was expecting him to do. Turn into a bat? Put on a cape and start speaking with a Transylvanian accent?

He got up from the chair, stepped over to the bed, and sat down next to me. He rested a hand on my knee. Staring me right in the eye (*I-know-what-you're-about*), he asked, "Are you sure?"

I was trembling. I was sure. "Yeah," I said.

He was going to kiss me, I thought. I'd asked him to prove he was a vampire, but seeing him stand up, dressed only in his underwear, obviously as excited as I was, and then watching him walk over and sit down next to me, and feeling his hand on my knee, I forgot all about the reason he was in such close proximity, or what I'd asked him to do. We were going to make out—maybe more—and it was going to be incredible. I wanted a kiss that would surpass even Brent Hartley's. I wanted a kiss that would knock Judy's hedge maze stunt right out of the ballpark of our crazy, competitive Olympics.

He put his other hand on my cheek. He turned my face toward his, and I closed my eyes.

But his lips didn't land on mine. They landed—no, his *teeth* landed—on my neck, his jaws open wide. I have to admit, it felt great and gave me goose bumps for a moment. Then he actually started to bite down, slowly, and I felt his incisors poking painfully into my flesh. There was a wetness on my neck (his spit? my blood?), and the clamp of his jaw was getting tighter. No exaggeration this time: It *hurt*.

I shoved him away.

"Come on!" he said in frustration. "I thought you were into me. I thought I was a sexy Bob Dylan."

At that moment, I didn't want him to be Bob Dylan *or* a vampire; I didn't even want him to be him—whoever he was.

"Do you want me to turn you into a vampire, or not? That's the only way to prove it!"

"I'm sick of all your posing!" I said, grabbing my shorts and pulling them back on. "It would be great if you'd be yourself, but I guess that's not going to happen. So I just want you to leave."

"Leave what? Your house? That's already going to happen soon enough."

"My *room*," I said, embarrassed and a little frightened. "And, yeah, my house. This is a sanctuary for genuine people, and only genuine people can be here. So get out." I don't know where the "sanctuary" business came from, but it worked. He got back into his clothes, collected his sketch pad and box of charcoals, and left the room without another word.

When he was gone, I walked over to the mirror hanging on the inside of my closet door and leaned into it, getting a good look at my neck. The skin wasn't broken, but where his incisors had been, there were four distinct indentations so deep, I don't know how he'd avoided drawing blood.

10. JUDY:
Pomp, circumstance, and a stab at the heart

I wore the church dress to Dexter's graduation ceremony. Dawn insisted on wearing her tinfoil elf ears. Trisha was willing to wear her best blouse and skirt, but wanted to add her light-up sneakers to the ensemble. Suzie wanted to wear the miniature red lacquered cowboy hat she'd won in a school raffle, and Tommy, who'd given up on his goatee but hadn't gotten a haircut since starting at U.Va., had just enough hair in the back to squeeze into a little nub of a ponytail that stuck straight out over his shirt collar and looked like the stem of a blow-up doll. Mom and Dad surrendered to them all, so long as none of them made us late.

"Look at you," Mom said to Dexter in his cap and gown, as we all stood in the driveway waiting for Dad to back the Yukon out of the garage. "Such a man. And just yesterday you were in diapers."

"Ha!" Dawn said, her ears crinkled and pointy, reflecting what little sunlight shone through the heavy, gray clouds. "Diapers!"

Dexter flipped Dawn the bird and Mom shushed her and smacked Dexter's hand down. "No fighting now. Not today. This is such a happy occasion, because Dexter's really accomplished something. It wasn't easy at times, was it? That physics class was a disaster. And your French teacher didn't do you any favors. But you did it: You're graduating." She let out a little sniffle.

"Oh, come on, Mom. Don't cry."

"I'm not crying. I have allergies." She pulled a tissue from her purse and brought it to her nose. "I just wish you were going to carry on your education."

"I am," Dexter said. "I've been waiting till today to tell you. I'm not taking the job at Athletic Mongoose; I'm going to U.Va. after all."

Tommy already knew this, I could tell. He cocked a finger at Mom playfully, as if maybe he'd had something to do with getting Dexter to change his mind.

"That's wonderful!" Mom said. "That's terrific news! What brought about the change of heart?"

"Just seemed like the wise thing to do," Dexter said.

"Plus," Tommy added, "I found out Beth Garland is headed off for Dartmouth at the end of the summer. Turns out she's a brainiac. Who would have guessed?"

"Who's Beth Garland?" Mom asked.

"The girl Dexter likes who works at Athletic Mongoose."

"*That's* what this whole 'no college' thing was about? A *girl?*" Mom asked in disbelief.

Dexter just shrugged and readjusted his mortarboard as he stepped out of the way of the Yukon.

The car was long and white, like a beluga whale. It was the most unlefty thing about Mom and Dad because it drank gas and killed the atmosphere, but they wanted at least one vehicle the whole family could fit into for occasions just like this. We did fit—but barely, with Garret added to the mix. (Mom had insisted he come along, and he was politely obliging.) Once we were all inside, Mom turned to Dad and said, "Dexter's decided he's going to U.Va. after all!"

"Wonderful!" Dad said, glancing into the rearview mirror. "Will you be living in the dorm?"

"Nah. I'm gonna commute, like Tommy," Dexter said.

"Oh." Dad glanced at Mom. "They'll never move out. None of them. We're stuck."

"Hush," Mom said.

We were just out of the driveway when it started to rain. *Pour* was more like it. You could barely see through the windshield, the water was splattering so hard against the glass, though Dad had the wipers going full speed.

I glanced behind me to the backseat, where Garret sat on one side, Kyle on the other, Trisha and her blinking shoes between them. Both Garret and Kyle were staring out their side windows, looking miserable. Had something happened between them? I was tempted to ask, but still felt too angry to want to talk to anyone. I was mad at Garret for ratting me out to Kyle, and at Kyle for being the happy recipient of the ratting, and at Jacob for not wanting to be my friend. I was mad at myself for hurting Sasha's feelings. And, to be honest, I'd lost track of just how much *I'd* done to help create all this mess, so I decided to stay quiet and just try to rubberhead it through the day.

Garret, I noticed, was as dressed up as I'd ever seen him. He was still wearing his eyeliner on one eye, but he had on new-looking black jeans and a black long-sleeved shirt, the sleeves buttoned around the cuffs. Kyle was wearing his navy blazer and khaki pants, and his good brown loafers. He actually looked handsome. More like a young man than a boy.

"This weather doesn't bode well for an outdoor ceremony," Dad said, leaning into the windshield so that he could see better. "Something tells me we're going to end up in the gym rather than the football stadium."

"I just hope they don't send the band home," Mom said. "I love hearing 'Pomp and Circumstance' live."

When we reached the school, there was no sign of anyone wielding musical instruments. Mr. Anderson, the senior class sponsor, had, in fact, sent the band home once the skies had opened up. He was a chubby, gray-faced man with white hair, and he was easily winded. As he and another teacher constructed a makeshift stage made out of risers, you could see his chest heaving and his white shirt turning the color of a peach from across the gym. We were filing along the back of the enormous room when I ran into Sasha—the first time I'd seen her since she'd stormed out of our house after telling me off.

"Hey," I said hesitantly. "Where's your oboe?"

"I put it back in the band room. They told us there wasn't enough space for us to play in here. Looks like there's plenty of space to me."

"Well, you can sit with us, if you want. We're all here to see Dexter wrap his meaty paw around that diploma and wave it in the air like a maniac."

"No, thanks," Sasha said without looking at me. "I have some friends I'm going to sit with, over there." She pointed in the general direction of the opposite side of the gym, and wandered off.

What *friends*? I couldn't see anyone over there who Sasha hung out with. Was she really not interested in knowing me anymore? Was I really the jerk she thought I was? How could I even know, at this point? Everything seemed to have fallen apart so fast. Everyone was suddenly so…sensitive.

I watched after her as I followed the family four rows up into the bleachers in procession. We sat down: a long line of Rennekers, with Garret at the far end of the row next to Kyle. For a while, there was nothing to do but watch one of the coaches yell at a half-dozen students (freshmen, no doubt) to move faster as they hastily set up row after row of folding chairs across the basketball court for the graduates to sit on. Once the chairs were set up, the graduates were arranged alphabetically and directed to take their seats.

The gym fell nearly silent as the principal, Ms. Rutledge, made her way up the steps and across the risers. She had her reading glasses on and an index card in her hand. Just as she was approaching the microphone, lightning flashed outside the high, screened windows, and thunder cracked overhead. People "oooed" and "aahhed" as if they were watching fireworks. "My," Ms. Rutledge said into the microphone. "How's that for a starting note?"

A few people clapped, which made a few other people laugh. Then she announced why we were all gathered here today, and the place erupted with hoots and howls—most of the noise, of course, coming from the graduates themselves.

"I'd just like to say that this class, in particular, shows great promise. I fully expect these graduates of Milton High to go on to do wonderful—even amazing—things. And I wish you all a happy, healthy future."

The content of the program was almost an exact replica of Tommy's graduation ceremony the year before, except that this year we were all crammed inside the gym instead of being out at the football stadium. Ms. Rutledge gave the same pep talk; Mr. Madison, the assistant principal, made the same joke about the recruit who thought boot camp was where you learned how to be a cobbler (yawn); the valedictorian, as far as I could tell, delivered the same "we can change the world" speech as the one given by last year's valedictorian (she even *looked* like the same girl). *Kyle and I will be going through this same thing next year,* I thought, glancing down at the sea of black mortarboarded heads. *We'll be sitting side by side, waiting for it all to be over, waiting to cross the platform and get our diplomas so we can wave them in the air and launch our hats and scream our heads off.* Then I surprised myself with an added thought: *It would be kind of nice if we were getting along when that happens.*

The ceremony dragged on and on, with a flash of lightning and a tremendous crash of thunder every now and then, giving the whole thing an ominous feel. As the graduates began to parade up and receive their diplomas, Mr. Anderson—how pathetic is this?—pulled out a little tape recorder, put in a cassette, hit PLAY, and held a microphone against the speaker. The tiniest little strands of "Pomp and Circumstance" started to drain through the PA system, as if a band of mice were playing miniature instruments under the bleachers. I looked at Mom, and she rolled her eyes.

Finally, they got to the *R*s and it was Dexter's turn to cross the risers. When Ms. Rutledge announced his name, Dawn and Suzie and Trisha started screaming as if they'd been set on fire. Mom, Dad, Tommy, and Kyle all clapped and hollered—even I joined in with a little noisemaking (I'm not made of stone, after all). As I did, I glanced down at Garret to see if he was taking part in the festivities. He was. At least, he was clapping with a glum look on his face—

—until the one student at Milton High who'd been banished from school grounds until further notice charged up the aisle to the end of the row where he was sitting and attacked him.

Not with a vial of holy water, not with a fake musket, but with a mallet in one hand and a wooden stake in the other.

"What the—" Garret said.

Kyle thought fast and stuck his foot out. Coover pitched forward—but into Garret, who twisted around and fell into the row behind him. Then two of the coaches charged up the aisle, held Coover down, and wrestled the implements out of his hands.

Mom asked, "What *hap*pened?" about five times in a row, because there were so many people around Garret now that she couldn't even see him from where she was standing. Then a bewildered Mr. Anderson dropped the microphone to the floor (not easy on the ears, as you can imagine).

"Order, please!" Ms. Rutledge called out, as if we were in a courtroom.

The good news—the fantastic news, actually, because let's face it, the situation could have been bloody, if not deadly—is that Ferris Coover never got the stake anywhere near Garret's chest. The bad news, as we later found out, was that Garret had sprained his ankle when he fell.

The poor Zephweiser twins. No one even looked, much less applauded, when they were handed their diplomas. All eyes were on the chaos down at our end of the gym, the rustle of voices in the absence of "Pomp and Circumstance," accented by thunderclaps and flashbulbs.

On the drive to the hospital, Mom called the Johnsons in San Diego and told them what had happened. They confirmed Garret's insurance information, and we took him into the emergency room and practically filled the waiting area, there were so many of us. Garret was pushed away in a wheelchair. He was obviously in a lot of pain, and no one made any sort of joke or even wisecrack about the attack, because we didn't know yet how severe his injury was. As soon as he was gone, Dad got back on the phone with Mr. Johnson.

"Yes, I know," Dad said. "That boy who attacked Garret needs some serious therapy. I was told he's already been seeing someone, but clearly something's not working. I'm sorry about this, Hal. . . . I know that, but I'm still sorry it happened on my watch. Garret's going to be fine, don't you worry. And as for the police, they were already at the school by the time we left, so . . . well, of course you can file your own report, if you'd like. I'm not quite sure how these situations work. . . ."

Things didn't look good for Coover, that much was certain.

Once the X-ray results were in, a nurse cut away the leg of Garret's pants and wrapped him from knee to toe in an ACE bandage. She gave him crutches, a pill for the pain (which almost immediately made him drowsy), and wrote a prescription for some more pain pills that Mom filled at the hospital pharmacy before we all filed back out to the car, Dad pushing the wheel-chair and Kyle carrying the crutches.

At home I made up the couch in the living room for Garret to lie down on, his bad ankle propped up on pillows. He was extra quiet, didn't seem to want to talk to any of us (other than his thanking Mom and Dad for looking after him), and as soon as he'd settled in, he was out like a light.

This may sound tacky, but Tommy, Dexter, Dawn, Suzie, and Trisha all took advantage of Garret's sudden confinement to the living room and went upstairs to enjoy the game room. Dad said he'd had enough drama for one day and needed to take a nap, and once the rain cleared up, Mom drove to the grocery store to buy food for Dexter's special-request graduation dinner: tacos and guacamole. Only Kyle and I remained in the living room, sitting in the recliners, leafing through magazines and watching Garret sleep.

His cell phone started bleating. My eyes met Kyle's, but neither one of us moved. It rang and rang, then went silent. A few moments later, it rang again. Again, we didn't move. When it rang for the fourth time, I set down my magazine, went over to the couch, and found it in one of the front pockets of his jeans.

"Hello?"

"Garret?" a woman's voice asked.

"No, this is Judy. Judy Renneker." *God*, I thought, *am I talking to his vampire trainer? What was her name—Helena?* "Garret's sleeping right now."

"Oh, the poor thing. I'm so worried about him. Hal and I are just beside ourselves, with this happening and us all the way out in California. We've met before, I think. I'm Garret's mom, Helen."

Helen, I thought. *Not Helena. Helen.* I felt like a piece of the puzzle was being snapped into place—or being pulled out of the picture. "Garret's fine. But the doctor gave him some pain pills and he's sort of knocked out."

"The poor thing," she said again. "I know he hates these adjustment periods. We thought it would be easier for him this time, having him stay there with your family so that he could finish out the school year. We had no idea something like *this* was going to happen."

"It was pretty intense. Um, can I ask you a question? Do you and Garret, you know, talk on a regular basis?" I asked, glancing at Kyle.

"Oh, yes," she said. "That's why I got him the phone. I didn't want to be tying up your line, and I wanted to keep in touch with him as much as possible while we're apart. And he's so funny. I can always tell when someone else is around when I call, because he says the silliest things. It's like some game he's playing, only I don't know what the game is."

"I've actually heard him say some of that crazy stuff."

"It's silly, right? I'll say, 'How's your schoolwork coming along?' and he'll say, 'I haven't bitten anyone lately.' I'm always on the other end of the line saying, 'Oh, stop it, sweetheart. Talk right,' but that just makes him do it more. When *he* calls *me*, it's different. That's when he's alone, I guess."

"He calls you?"

"All the time. And then he's his normal self. Saying he misses me and his father, and telling me how nice you all are being to him, of course. Hal and I are *awfully* appreciative of what your family's done for him. He's really felt welcome there."

"Well, sorry it had to end this way. That kid who attacked him has some major problems."

"It certainly sounds like it. And I hear he's in trouble with the police now. Hal wants to press charges, but I told him we should let it go. It can't happen again—not to Garret, anyway, because he won't be there—and as long as that boy gets help..."

"He definitely needs it," I said.

We talked for another few minutes, she thanked me about a dozen more times, and we hung up. I set the cell phone on the coffee table and looked at Kyle. "That was 'Helena,'" I told him.

Kyle's eyes widened. "The Lestat woman?"

"Her name's Helen, actually. She's Garret's mom."

"Wait." Kyle let his magazine fall into his lap. "That was his *mom* he was having all those wacky conversations with?"

"Apparently they were only wacky from his end. She said she always knew when one of us was around, because he'd go into his routine. She had no idea what he was talking about."

You could see the wheels turning in Kyle's head, trying to figure things out. "So that means..."

"Of course," I said. "We already knew *that* much. Only Coover was screwy enough not to figure it out."

"Why do you think he does it? Garret, I mean. What does he get out of pretending?"

"I have no idea. But it hooked me for a while, I have to admit."

"Me, too," Kyle said.

"And you know what?" I lowered my voice to a whisper, just in case Garret woke up. "I don't even like him that much."

Kyle lowered his own voice. "Well, *I* do. If you don't like him, why were you going after him?"

"I wasn't going after him!" I hissed. "Well, okay, I was. And it's not that I *dis*like him; I just didn't care that much. I was after Jacob, really."

"Not much success in that department, I take it?"

"Stick to the topic," I said, motioning toward the figure sleeping on the couch. "I was only trying to win Garret because I knew you wanted him."

"*Why?* I mean, why does there always have to be this big competition between us?"

I walked back over to my recliner, sat down, and swiveled it from side to side with my feet. "I don't know, Kyle. I just can't help it. It's built into my brain, somehow. It's what I do."

"But only with me," he said. "You aren't like that with Dexter, or Dawn, or any of the others. Why do you hate me so much? Is it because I'm gay?"

"No."

"Well, why, then? I can't figure it out. Ever since you and Dad and Dexter moved out for that year, and then moved back in, you've acted like you can't stand me."

This was weird. We'd *never* had this kind of conversation before. I was both glad we were finally talking about it openly and over-the-top uncomfortable. I stopped moving the chair, pulled my feet up onto it, and bit at my thumbnail. After what felt like a long, awkward stretch of time, I said, "I don't *hate* hate you. But you really hurt my feelings once."

"What are you talking about?"

"Remember when Mom and Dad made their big announcement that they were splitting up?"

"Of course. Like it was yesterday."

"Well, the first thing that went through my head was, who's going to live where? I mean, how's this going to work? Are we going to draw straws, or what? And when I asked you about it, you said you didn't care."

"No, I didn't!"

"Yes, you did, Kyle. I asked who you thought was going to live with Mom and who with Dad and you practically sneered at me and said, 'I couldn't care less.'"

His jaw moved to one side as he ransacked his memory. I was quoting him directly, and I think he realized it. "I was *upset*, Judy. I was *mad* and...and really *sad*. I didn't want Mom and Dad to split up."

"Well, neither did I! Neither did any of us. But it didn't seem to make any difference to you whether you went off with

Dad or stayed with Mom, or whether I went off to live on the moon!"

"That wasn't how I felt."

"It *seemed* that way. And you know what? I *really* wanted to stay here. In this house, with Mom. I really wanted to stay here with *you*."

"Are you serious? You should have said something."

"To be honest, I didn't feel like saying anything after you told me that. But it wouldn't have mattered, anyway," I said, "They decided for us. For all we know, *they* drew straws to decide who went where. But the point is, you just didn't seem to care at all about where I ended up. And you lost interest in me, once I went off to live with Dad."

"How was I supposed to show interest in you? I wasn't even *around* you!"

"We spent weekends together, didn't we?" I asked, feeling upset in a way that surprised me. "You just checked out, as far as I could tell. You never seemed glad to see me, and you had this great big house to run around in, while I was stuck in that little dump of an apartment Dad rented...."

"So you were jealous."

"That was part of it, yeah. And maybe that's why I'm so competitive now. But the main thing was that you practically stopped being my brother for a whole year."

"That was the worst year of my life," he admitted. He was shaking his head, tapping into some pretty private stuff himself, I could tell. "I was really mad at Mom and Dad for splitting up. It just seemed so stupid. And I got, I don't know, depressed—if an eleven-year-old can get depressed."

"I think so," I said. "I'll bet even *babies* can get depressed."

"I didn't even have much to do with Tommy. It's not like we were having some big party over here without you guys. Maybe I didn't know how to show it, but if you want to know the truth, I really missed you. When I found out Mom and Dad were getting back together and you guys were moving back in, I was like, *yes.* And then you got here and acted like you didn't like me anymore."

"Well..." My eyes were tearing up. Kyle could see it, but that was okay because his own eyes looked a little glassy. "I didn't. Only because I thought you didn't care if I lived or died.".

"Jesus, that is so screwed up!" Kyle said. "Of course I care if you live or die! You're my sister!"

I wiped my eyes before the waterworks started running down my cheeks. "Thanks for saying that."

"Why didn't we ever just talk about all this stuff?"

"I don't know. We were kids."

"We're *still* kids, aren't we?"

I shrugged. "We're sixteen. Sometimes it doesn't feel like we're kids anymore. Which is great, in a way, but it's also pretty freaky."

We both fell silent. For a while the only sound in the room was Garret's steady breathing.

Kyle rocked in his recliner and tapped the magazine against his legs. He said, "Can we stop?"

"Stop what?"

"Competing, for one thing. It's really annoying."

I nodded. "Sure."

"And can we...I don't know...make some kind of deal? I'll make it really clear to you that I *do* care if you live or die, and *where* you live, and how I missed the hell out of you for that whole awful year, and you'll stop acting like you hate me?"

My eyes were still damp, but I felt myself smiling. I nodded again and said, "Done."

"Good," he said. "And I want you to stop calling me all those gay-joke names. You know, like 'The Boy Who Loves Penises.'"

"You know I don't care that you're gay."

"I know. So—knock it off. You think I like hearing that stuff all the time, even if you don't mean it?"

Listening to him, it struck me that we'd already made progress; I couldn't *imagine* calling him any of those names now. "Okay," I said. "But I want you to stop calling me Monster."

"As long as you stop being one."

"I said I'll stop!"

"Okay," he said. "Never again."

We sat there for a while with this new air hanging between us. I looked over at Garret's sleeping form and said, "I guess waiting hand and foot on our houseguest is going to be added to somebody's chore list."

"I guess so."

"The task should be assigned to someone who likes him, of course."

"That makes sense," Kyle said.

"Someone who *really* likes him."

"Uh-huh."

"Hey," I said, grinning at him as I stretched out my legs and opened up the recliner, lying back, "guess what?"

He gave me a cautious look, as if bracing for a nasty remark.

"You win."

11. KYLE:
Days of our
abbreviated lives

Judy left the room not long after letting me know I'd "won"
Garret. I stayed there, watching him sleep with his elevated,
ice-packed ankle, wondering what, exactly, I'd won. The last
time we'd spoken, I'd thrown him out of my room after telling
him he wasn't a genuine person. He'd said he was interested in
me, but he was moving to the other side of the country in a few
days. I'd been expecting a kiss, and he'd bitten my neck nearly
hard enough to break the skin.

I was on the verge of heading upstairs to my room to call Ian
and tell him the latest drama (just in case he hadn't already
heard about it) when Garret's eyes fluttered open.

He looked at the ceiling for a little while. Then he looked
down at his leg and the ice pack. Finally, he turned his head to
the side and gazed at me, where I sat in one of the recliners. "I
didn't dream that, did I?" he asked. "It really happened?"

"Coover attacking you with a wooden stake and a mallet at the graduation ceremony? Yeah, that really happened."

"*God,*" he said, and rubbed his eyes with both hands.

"How's the pain?"

"It's back, actually. Can I have another pill yet?"

I looked at the clock sitting on the end table. "Sure. Knock yourself out. Actually, don't. I'd kind of like to talk to you, if you're up for it."

"Okay." He groaned as he tried to sit upright, adjusting the pillows beneath his head. "As long as I don't have to stand to do it."

I got up and went into the kitchen, poured him a glass of water, and got him a pill from the bottle on the counter. "Here," I said, handing them both to him. When he'd rubbed his eyes, I noticed, he'd smeared his eyeliner. His left eye looked like it had been punched. I sat down on the edge of the coffee table.

"Thanks." He swallowed the pill, then gulped down the rest of the water.

"Your mom called while you were asleep. She called a few times, I think. Judy finally answered your phone and talked to her."

"Oh," he said in a drug-heavy voice. "What was that like?"

"Let's just say we cleared up the whole 'Helena' mystery."

"Helena is Helen, yes."

"And she's your mom, and not your 'Lestat.'"

"Right. The cat's out of the bag, I get it. But wait—you said

Coover had what? A stake and a mallet? It all happened so fast, I couldn't tell *what* he was up to."

"A *wooden* stake," I clarified. "The kind that might kill a vampire? In the movies, at least?"

"Ugh." He rubbed his eyes again. "I think I'm done being a vampire for a while."

I thought I'd feel relieved, finally hearing him admit it was all an act, but instead I just felt sorry for him. "Tell me something."

He groaned again. "Be kind."

"Why not just be a regular guy and make friends?"

"*God*, my ankle hurts."

"That doesn't answer my question."

"I know. But it still hurts." He laid his head back on the pillow and scratched at his scalp. His hair stood up in dark, crazy spikes. "You asked me once how I felt about moving to a new state every year, and I didn't answer because I didn't feel like talking about it. But now I guess I should."

"I'm all ears."

He winced and then exhaled loudly. "Well, imagine what that's like. Imagine starting every school year at a new school. Sometimes *switching* schools — and states — in the middle of the year. I never get to know *any*body for very long. Get it? If you know you're about to be hauled off to another state in twelve months or less, what's the point of trying to make really good friends? Not to mention trying to find a *boyfriend*."

"Boyfriend? You don't strike me as the kind of guy who's looking for a boyfriend."

"I'm not, because I *can't* be. Of course, I *want* a boyfriend, just like I want good, long-lasting friends. But I don't stand a chance at having either one, given my situation. With my dad's job, it's worse than being an army brat. At least *they* get to stick around a place for a few years at a time. But if you're me, you get to know people, and you start to like them, and then, bam, you're gone. It sucks."

"Sounds like it," I said.

"So you start finding ways to insulate yourself. Some balance between getting a little attention and keeping people at arm's length. Does that make sense? I just got here and I'm practically gone already."

"You and Judy have strange ways of dealing with your problems," I said—not that I was any problem-solving expert.

"I can't speak for her. All I know is, if there's a handbook for my situation, I wish someone would give me a copy."

"I still don't get it. If you wanted to keep *me* at arm's length, why'd you try to get me out of my clothes the other night?"

"Correction," he said sleepily, "I *did* get you out of your clothes the other night. Or most of them, anyway."

"But why? You certainly weren't at arm's length when you were biting my neck."

"That was hot." His eyes were closing.

I didn't want him to drift back off. Not yet. I reached out and took hold of his shoulder and shook it. "Don't fall asleep, asshole."

He looked up. *"Asshole?"*

"Sorry. That slipped out. But I really want to know: Why were you coming on to me?"

"Because I think you're great. I didn't at first—I mean, I didn't think *any*thing because I didn't pay any attention. And then by the time I realized I was into you, the whole vampire thing was already pretty much in place, so I had to go with it."

"You think I'm great?"

"Come on. You're fine with being who you are; you have this whole guitar thing going on, which is pretty sexy; you have this crazy obsession with Bob Dylan—I don't quite get it, but it's adorable—and you couldn't be any cuter if you tried."

For a moment, my brain stopped dead in its tracks. Somebody was actually into me? And that somebody was Garret Johnson?

"But you said it yourself. You're practically gone already. So why—"

"Look, you want to be a rock star, right?" he asked.

"I never said that."

"Admit it. You like the idea of being up on a stage, playing your guitar in front of people who are cheering you on."

He was right, of course; I gave him the slightest shrug to confirm it.

"And you can't *be* a rock star right now."

"What's your point?"

"My point is, you still enjoy playing your guitar, don't you?"

"So you 'played' me like I play my guitar?"

"That didn't come out the way I wanted it to. My point is, it was nice to at least fantasize for a few seconds that you were my boyfriend. But I still had the whole vampire thing to maintain. I mean, I've got to save face, right?"

Thinking about both his and Judy's predicaments—granted, predicaments I could never picture myself in in a million years—I knew what he meant. And I could think of about ten ways to turn what he was saying into an insult. But it was also a compliment, and I decided to take it that way. I said, "Maybe if you didn't go around claiming to be a vampire, people might *want* to be your friend, and might want to keep in touch with you after you move."

"Doesn't happen," he said, staring again at the ceiling.

"It *could* happen."

"Well, I guess it might—in San Diego. Fresh start, all that. I could just try being a boring old —"

"Mortal?"

He let out a soft, sleepy laugh. "Yeah."

"Well..." I scooted forward a little on the coffee table so that I was closer to him. "...I was thinking, it could maybe happen now, with *me*. We could try, anyway."

His head moved back on the pillow as if he needed a better look at who he was talking to. "You'd be interested in staying friends with me, after all this?"

"Yeah," I said. "If you'd just be *yourself.* If you'd stop with the head games and just be Garret."

"Garret is about to be living in California," he reminded me.

"And we have plenty of ways to communicate. We've got phones, and email, and IMing—if Judy'll let me on her laptop. And there are these things called airplanes, and sometimes people get on them and take trips and visit their friends."

"Okay, okay," he said. "Point taken."

"I really want to like you," I said. "I mean, I *do* like you. *This* you. The one who's being honest with me. If I could keep knowing the real you, I'd like that. I'd like that a lot, in fact."

He nodded. I saw his tongue tracing the inside of his cheek as he thought about it. "Me, too," he said.

For what felt like nearly a full minute we just looked at each other. Then I said, "This is driving me crazy," and went to lick my finger. I stopped and held the finger close to his mouth instead. "Give me some spit."

His gaze widened a little. "Why?"

"Your eyeliner. You've smeared it all over the place; it looks like you have a black eye."

Looking right at me, grinning, he took my finger into his mouth and moistened it.

Yes, I was flirting. I admit it, okay? But at least I wasn't pretending to be something other than who I was while I was doing it. I was me, Kyle Renneker, dealing with the situation as best I could. And enjoying myself a little. Well, enjoying myself a *lot*, once he took my finger into his mouth. He closed his left eye, and I rubbed at it gently, but all the rubbing did was spread the eyeliner farther down his cheek. "Don't move," I told him, getting up.

"Don't worry."

I went into the kitchen and wet a paper towel at the sink, then carried it back into the living room and knelt down next to him. He closed his eye again while I rubbed away the eyeliner. When I was finished, he leaned forward suddenly, his mouth opening, and this time he wasn't going for my neck.

It didn't feel like cooked pasta shells rubbing together, and it didn't feel like a jolt of electricity slamming through my body. It just felt... fantastic.

He was a little more mobile the next day. And a little more the day after that. He experimented with walking around the first floor of the house on his crutches, which went fine until the blood started pounding in his foot and he had to elevate it again. But as it turns out, a recliner is the perfect chair for someone with a sprained ankle. So there he was, in our living room around the clock, present and accounted for instead of hiding away in the attic between mealtimes or in the evenings. He watched TV with Dexter and Tommy. He taught Dawn how to use charcoal to shade dark to light, taught her how to use her finger to smudge in the right places. Suzie taught him how to play gin rummy, and beat him every time (he was letting her win, I suspected). It was great seeing so much of him and watching him interact with everyone, but at the same time, I wanted to be alone with him now more than ever.

"Have you two kissed again?" Ian asked me over the phone after I'd given him a full update.

"Maybe I'm not the kind who tells," I said.

"Right. You're the kind who announces it through a bullhorn. *Have you?*"

"Yeah, we have. But it hasn't been easy because he's basically camped out on the first floor, which may as well be Grand Central, so we haven't been able to be by ourselves, except for, like, two seconds at a time."

"Poor you," Ian said.

"Hey, *poor me* is right. He's leaving in less than a week! And now that he's not a vampire anymore, I *really* like him."

"Who would have thought Ferris Coover would ever do you such a favor? If he hadn't flaked out at graduation, you and Garret might never have taken this big romantic step."

"*That's* an exaggeration," I said. "We're not romantic. We haven't had sex or even come close to it. I told you, he's staying in the living room. We've just made out a few times."

"It's very Hemingway. It's very nurse-and-wounded-soldier-falling-in-love-during-wartime."

"I'm not his nurse. I'm his friend."

"Whatever, Miss Nightingale. Oh—and if I sound jaded and jealous? It's only because I am."

I laughed. "You're too young to be jaded."

"I'm working on it," he said. "Jaded, depraved, and deflowered — they're all on my list."

We figured out one way to clear the room. We pretended to take interest in a soap opera — *Days of Our Lives* — and *none* of them wanted to watch it, especially not when there was a game room in the attic. The show would come on, they would groan, and then they'd head upstairs to watch a movie or play air hockey and video games. We managed some nice make-out sessions while listening for footsteps coming down the stairs. Not that we were trying to hide the fact that we'd taken an interest in each other; we just didn't want to lip-lock in front of them. (I certainly wouldn't have wanted to watch any of *them* lip-lock with somebody.)

Judy — ex-fake-Christian — performed the ultimate ironic act by surprising the hell out of me when, one day just as the soap opera was starting, she presented us with a picnic lunch she'd prepared all by herself. It was in a basket she'd found in the garage and lined with a red-checkered cloth. There were sandwiches, chips, cookies, apples, and two bottles of soda.

"Wow," I said. "Thanks. What's the occasion?"

"Well, I'm trying out this random-act-of-kindness thing. Weird, huh?"

"Very."

"Enjoy," she said, and started for the front door.

"Where are you off to?"

"I'm going over to Sasha's to see if I can convince her I'm not the big jerk she thinks I am."

"Why does she think you're a jerk?"

"It's a long story," Judy said. "And I *was* a jerk. I just don't feel like one anymore, and I want to see if I have a chance of proving it."

"Good luck with that," I said.

She had her hand on the doorknob. She stopped and whipped her head around, as if she thought I was being sarcastic.

"Really," I said. "I hope it goes well. You guys have been friends a long time. You should patch things up, if there's trouble."

"Thanks." She didn't smile but gave me a very serious and, I thought, appreciative look. "I'll let you know how it goes."

Then she left, the commercials ended, and the first scene of the program began. Garret and I turned away from the screen. (We had no idea what was going on in the show and didn't care; we wanted to make out and eat sandwiches.)

He asked me, in one of our private, soap-opera-encased moments, if I'd ever had sex before. I gave him an abbreviated version of the Brent Hartley story, then said, "What about you?"

"Yes, actually. With a girl."

"You had sex with a girl? Who was it?"

"Kara Thurston. I was living in Wisconsin and she was my next-door neighbor. We were both fourteen."

"Wow. How did that go?"

He shrugged. "It was interesting."

"Nice description," I said.

"How about you? Ever had sex with a girl?"

"No. I could say it was just because the opportunity never presented itself, but the truth is, I never really *wanted* it to present itself." He was wearing shorts and I was sitting on the floor next to his recliner, rubbing a hand over the exposed knee of his good leg. "I've pretty much known what I like from the get-go."

"Lucky for me, then," he said and pushed his leg against my hand.

"Hey," I said impulsively, "maybe I'll pretend to be a zombie when the new school year starts. See if I can get Coover all riled up again."

"Don't joke about that," Garret said. "Even if they get that guy the right counseling and the right medication, I don't want you taking any chances around him—especially if I'm not here to help protect you. For all we know, he'll have just rented *I Am Legend* and will try to blast you away with a machine gun."

"You'd protect me?"

"Of course. I'd want to—and the least I can do is return the favor, right?"

"What favor?" I asked.

"You tripped Coover. You might have saved my life."

"Yeah, but I think tripping Coover was what made you

sprain your ankle. You might not have fallen if I hadn't stuck my foot out and made him fall into you."

"True," he said. "But I'll take the sprained ankle any day."

I smiled at him. I moved in to give him a kiss, then stopped short. "How did you know I tripped Coover? Nobody mentioned it, as far as I know, and I didn't say anything because I thought I'd only made things worse."

"Judy told me all about it," he said. "Told me I owed you big-time."

Every once in a while, life rocks. On the morning of Garret's departure, Mom pointed out that, because of his convalescence, it had been days since he'd had a shower, and didn't he want to be clean for his reunion with his parents?

"I guess that's not a bad idea," he said.

Then she asked if I would be willing to help him.

"H-help him?"

"Make it up the stairs," she said. "And maybe set a stool in the shower, and help him get in and out, so he can bathe without having to stand on one leg."

Garret tapped my shoulder. "That doesn't sound like such a bad idea, either."

She had the slightest smile in her mouth, waiting for me to respond. She knew exactly what she was doing, and that, in my book, makes her the greatest mom in the entire history of this or any other universe—*no* exaggeration.

"Okay," I said.

I guided him upstairs, all the way to the attic, where we locked the door behind us, got out of our clothes, carefully unwrapped his ankle, and had quite a good time soaping him up — okay, soaping each other up — in a shower that lasted long enough to deplete the entire house of hot water.

Fortunately, none of the others could join Mom, Garret, and me on the trip to the airport in Richmond. Dad had patients lined up and said his good-byes before leaving the house that day. Judy had plans to go shopping with Sasha at the mall (apparently their friendship was at least starting to be on the mend). Tommy and Dexter were venturing into the world of paintball at a new place that had opened two towns over, and both Suzie and Trisha wanted Dawn to show them what Garret had taught her about shading and smudging charcoal.

It was a quiet hour and a half in the car. Mom drove, we sat in the backseat, and Garret reached over at one point and gave my hand a squeeze. I squeezed his back, and didn't let go of it for miles.

Inside the airport, as we were nearing the security area, Mom said, "Oh, gosh, I forgot to get a copy of *Vogue*. Garret, I'm going to say good-bye to you here and run back to that newsstand we just passed. You have a safe flight, and call us when you get to San Diego."

"Will do," he said, shaking her hand. "Thanks for everything, Mrs. R."

"My pleasure. Kyle, I'll be right over there."

She walked off toward the newsstand.

I grinned at Garret. "She doesn't read *Vogue*."

"Very cool of her."

"I know."

"So, listen," he said, "it's been a strange month, to say the least, but…"

For the first time since I'd met him, he seemed to be at a loss for words. So I kissed him: right in front of the security guards.

"Call me," I said. "Tonight."

"Definitely," he said.

He surrendered his backpack, his wallet, and his belt to a plastic tray. They let him keep his single shoe, but they X-rayed his crutches, making him hop through the metal detector on one foot. When he was put back together, he twisted around and looked back to where I was standing alone against the wall. He gave a little wave. I gave a big one.

Then he was gone.

12. JUDY:
Last notes from the Mean Front (sort of)

Witnessing someone else's graduation from Milton High was sort of like seeing a stranger win a car on a game show. But let me tell you: Walking across that platform myself a year later, with Kyle right behind me, was *awesome*. And I'm happy to say our ceremony was not only attack-free, but sunny! It took place in the football stadium, with the band going full blast (Mom was pleased). Dad filmed the event with his new camcorder and then played it back for us on the wide-screen TV in the game room, and of course he was narrating with great fanfare the whole time he was filming, as if anyone but our family was ever going to watch the footage: "And there's Ms. Judy Renneker now! That's my daughter, folks, yes, sir, and I'm bursting with pride. Doesn't she look gorgeous—and smart! Oh, and there's Kyle! Kyle Renneker, third mortarboard down from the end of the aisle. My youngest son is quite a handsome devil, if I do say so myself, and he gets that from me (chuckle). Of course, Kyle's the one with a gift for exaggeration, so he'd probably tell me I'm out-of-my-mind insane for saying that!"

"Honey," Mom said, "did you talk through the whole ceremony?"

"It's a documentary," Dad said. "I facilitated the story."

She rolled her eyes.

Then there was a close-up shot of Dawn sitting about a foot away from Dad. She'd gotten over her aluminum foil fixation by then and had moved on to multicolored rubber bands; she had about thirty of them wound around her hair so that she looked like some sort of punk rock child, and she was really hamming it up, mugging for the camera. The big-screen TV made her head look enormous. "And what do we have here?" Dad asked, filming her.

"Me."

"And just what are you supposed to be?"

"I'm *supposed* to be Dawn," she said, which I thought was hilarious.

And the funniest part of all: When Kyle and I were standing together on the platform with our diplomas in our hands and waving up to where the folks sat (Mom had specifically instructed us to do this), Dad tried to applaud and film at the same time and dropped the camera, so the whole picture went *whoosh* and there was this loud thud, and suddenly all we were looking at on the TV screen was the side of his shoe. He picked the camera back up and turned it on himself. "Sorry about that, folks. A little technical difficulty here in the studio, but all is well. Rest assured: No one was attacked!"

"An Oscar winner you're not," Mom told him as we watched the footage.

"You can't fault me for trying," he replied, and she leaned over and kissed the side of his head.

By then, Kyle and I had both been accepted to U.Va. The letters arrived on the same day, and we sat across from each other at the kitchen table and tore into them. I don't know what we were thinking, because it would have been horrible if one of us had gotten in and the other hadn't. (Talk about a moment that would have sparked up that whole "competition" thing.) I held my letter up to my face and scanned it quickly, then peeked around the edge to get a look at Kyle. He was smiling, and we both exhaled, then jumped up from our chairs and started screaming like kids.

He also got into Virginia Commonwealth, and I managed to get into the University of Richmond (which was a surprise, since I'd been told that their entire student body was imported from New Jersey), but we both ultimately decided on U.Va.

Tommy and Dexter were living there now. They'd moved into an apartment together at the beginning of their spring semester—much to Dad's relief, though he'd gotten all misty-eyed once we'd finished loading their cars and they were rolling down the driveway. Mom told him to stop or he'd get her crying, too, and then a second later the tears were rolling down her cheeks.

"Mine are tears of joy," Dad said. "I thought they'd never leave." But we all knew he didn't mean it.

"My twins," Mom said, glancing at me and Kyle where we stood on the front porch, "you're next."

It was *almost* a funny moment because it sounded like a threat, as if she were threatening to fire us from our jobs. But I knew what she meant: It wasn't just that we were next in line, it was that everything seemed to be happening so fast.

She'd taken our diplomas to the frame shop on the Monday following the ceremony, and a week later they were hanging alongside Tommy's and Dexter's in the foyer, with open wall space next to them for Dawn's, Suzie's, and Trisha's. Their diplomas were years away, of course, but they somehow felt just around the corner.

Among all the other stuff I learned during senior year—from teachers and books—I also learned what I like to call a Lesson in Love (and I don't care how corny that sounds). It went like this:

Right after classes started, I met a cute boy named Marcus Brock, who had a wiry body, sandy-blond hair, and big plans to be an architect. He carried around scrolls of blueprints for buildings he wanted to construct: condominiums and resorts and business parks. All the lines were drawn with a special drafting pencil and labeled with measurements. Within a few days of meeting him, I checked out books from the library on Frank Lloyd Wright and Antoni Gaudí and began sketching building plans of my own to try to impress him.

My plans looked ridiculous. The ones based on Wright looked like cereal boxes stacked on top of one another (with the occasional waterfall), and the ones based on Gaudí looked like pregnant fish left to die on a beach. I thought, *Am I nuts? I don't know anything about designing a building—and I don't care!*

I dropped the act almost before it began, never mentioned any interest in architecture to him, and you know what? He still wanted to hang out with me, and *he* made the first move—a goodnight kiss on our front porch. How romantic is *that*?

Right after that kiss—I mean, like, one second after our lips parted—I asked him in a nice way, "Why'd you do that?"

He said, "Because I like you, Judy."

Not *Judy Fill-in-the-Blank-with-Whatever-You're-Pretending-to-Be*. He liked me for *me*.

So I said, "And I like you, Marcus."

He kissed me again, asked me out the following Saturday, and we've been dating ever since.

Oh—and just in case you're dying of curiosity, I'll tie up a few loose ends:

Brent Hartley—the tennis player with the nice legs who I once had a crush on? The one Sasha mentioned when she was making fun of me for carrying around a tennis racket?—

transferred from U.Va. to Georgetown and, from what Tommy reports (via a friend who's a junior there), is now head of the Christian Student Alliance. When I told Kyle, he about fell out of his chair laughing.

"What's so funny?" I asked.

"Sorry," Kyle said, composing himself. "I'm just having a private moment."

His friend Ian Heller did just what he always said he was going to do: He moved to New York City a few weeks after graduating from Milton High. He's living up there now with some uncle nobody had ever heard him mention before: Uncle Leo—on his mom's side? His dad's? We didn't ask, though my secret theory is that he met this "uncle" online in some chat room the minute he got to New York, or maybe even before he left Milton. Ian emails Kyle now about how he might apply to Hunter College, or might apply to Columbia, but how all he's really interested in is swimming. He swims and swims and swims, every day. In one email (Kyle forwarded it to me with a subject line that read: *!!!!!*), Ian attached a photo of himself wearing nothing but a Speedo, and he looked skinny and muscular in all the right places. He even had a decent haircut, for a change. So good for Ian and Uncle Leo (I guess).

And Sasha! This one you won't believe; it even knocked me for a loop.

We're friends again, mainly because she let herself tell me off about a month into restarting our friendship. I was stupid enough to observe that her laugh sounded like a vacuum sucking up Jell-O cubes, and she blurted, "You know what? I just wish I could tell you off when you make cracks like that. I just wish I could make myself insult you right back!"

"So do it," I said. "With my blessing."

And she let me have it in a way that made our science test study session look like a lovefest. I mean, that girl can *swear* when she wants to! It was all stuff she'd hinted at the last time we'd had a fight, but apparently she was much angrier than she'd let on before, and needed to get a lot of stuff off her chest. Once she'd done that (about a half hour later), she was fine, I was fine, and now *we're* fine—I think.

But that isn't the surprising part. What knocked me for a loop is that she applied for some mondo-competitive, international junior banking internship in Spain...and *got it.* She's living in Madrid now! The emails she sends me are just as flighty as ever ("You should see the boys here, they're all so sexy and Spanish!!"), but apparently, the girl's got a brain in that head of hers. Who knew?

The last word anyone heard about Ferris Coover is that he was carted off to live on his grandparents' farm in Kentucky. He's milking cows, or collecting eggs, and is probably eyeing the chickens sideways, sniffing for signs of "the dark side." Or maybe it's helping, being out on a farm and away from everyone else's craziness. I hope so.

As for Kyle and Garret, they're long-distance boyfriends who send constant emails to each other (Kyle's on the laptop now more than I am) and what they call "hot texts." I don't know how it can possibly last with so many miles between them, but Kyle's happy as can be because he's flying out to San Diego later in the summer and spending a whole week nonstop in Garret's arms—or so he says. (They have to let go of each other some-time, right? To go to the bathroom, at least?)

I'm happy for him. I don't make fun of him for the gay thing anymore. And he hasn't called me Monster in over a year. Our clearing the air felt like something we should have done a lot sooner—like, six years sooner—because Kyle really is a pretty cool brother and it was just so useless, my being grouchy around him and staying mad at him for something he hadn't even meant to do.

Ever think you'd hear me being so nice? It's the new me. I swear! I'm Miss Friendly now. Miss Have a Nice Day. I was voted "Most Kindhearted Person at Milton High" in the year-book. Okay, I wasn't; the category doesn't exist. But if it did, I at least could have been in the running.

Seriously—and trust me on this—if you have a sibling you think you don't like: Try anything you can to start liking them again. Get whatever it is out in the open; clear the air. I know I'm only seventeen but, still, life is short. And being mean? It takes energy. As in, you wake up in the morning and you've got only so much energy for the day, and being mean just sucks it right out of you. It's *exhausting*.

As for the Renneker world in general, the house is quieter and, of course, emptier now that both Tommy and Dexter have moved out. And it's going to settle down even more once Kyle and I go off to college in August. For as chaotic and loud as the old homestead could get, I have to say I'm glad I *won't* be there to see it calm down another couple of notches, because it just won't be the same. Crazy to think that one day it will just be Trisha there, living with Mom and Dad. And crazier still to think that one day it will just be Mom and Dad: alone, in that big airplane hangar of a house. Maybe they'll sell the place. I hope not, though. I'd miss it.

Oh, and one last thing:

Jacob Lindsey? He got Tina pregnant! They had a shotgun wedding, she popped out triplets, put on a *lot* of weight, and for some reason lost all her teeth. He's got a beer gut now and they live in a trailer next to the junkyard on Crescent Road (the *wrong* side of the wrong side of the tracks). Some nights the police have to be called out because they have these loud fights and smash things up and shoot pistols into the air.

Okay, none of that is true (but wouldn't it be funny if it were?). As far as I know, they're still dating and are as happy as two peas in a bible, and I say good for them.

Ish.

(I suppose the "being nice" thing should be considered a work in progress. Nobody's perfect...right?)

So the only big question facing me now is the one Sasha put in my head right when I was in the middle of Crisis Central: What do I want to be when I grow up? And I've decided to take her advice, since she's proven herself to be a brainiac: I'm going to go one step at a time, and major in switching majors. At least for a year or so. Because if people can go from vampires to being boyfriend material, and from would-be monster-slayers to cow-milkers, and from Monster to Miss Congeniality, well, anything's possible, right? And why waste right now trying to figure it all out?

ACKNOWLEDGMENTS

Thank you to David Levithan and to Lisa Bankoff for having faith in this story and helping it see the light of day. Thank you to Sandy McInerny, who first encouraged me to write. And immeasurable gratitude to the one and only Fred Blair, who not only puts up with but encourages me.